CONVERGENCE

FLASHPOINT BOOK 5

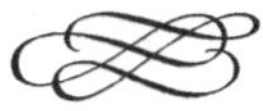

TARA ELLIS

MIKE KRAUS

MUONIC PRESS

CONVERGENCE
The Flashpoint Series
Book 5

By
Tara Ellis
Mike Kraus

CONTENTS

WANT MORE AWESOME BOOKS?

Find more fantastic tales at books.to/readmorepa.

If you're new to reading Mike Kraus, consider visiting his website at MikeKrausBooks.com and signing up for his free newsletter. You'll receive several free books and a sample of his audiobooks, too, just for signing up, you can unsubscribe at any time and you will receive absolutely *no* spam.

You can also stay updated on Tara's books by following her Facebook page: www.facebook.com/taraellisauthor

SPECIAL THANKS

Special thanks to my awesome beta team, without whom this book wouldn't be nearly as great.

Thank you!

PREFACE

As paths cross and lives collide, the question of what it means to survive is confronted, whether the answer is wanted or not.

The dust continues to settle from the destruction of the gamma-ray burst, and new challenges arise in its wake. Some of the obstacles are obvious, while others are more insidious and require a tenacity to defeat that few possess.

Tom and his son, Ethan, have come together with Danny and her friend, Sam, and continued their trek together. They're about to reach their hometown in Mercy, Montana. After more than two weeks on the run, they've each overcome their own battles to get there. The wounds from those conflicts might leave some scars and although reaching safety is a relief, it's also yet another unknown. What's been happening in Mercy since the flashpoint, and how will they fit in?

Mayor Patty is struggling to feel at home, even though she's supposed to be the one running things in Mercy. With one challenge after another hurled at her, what's right and wrong isn't clear, and neither is her conscience.

Chloe has thrown herself into farm life with both feet and is determined to make her way in the new world. But if the teen thought she struggled to get along with people before everything got turned upside-down, it was nothing compared to what she's facing now. While juggling to keep her current friends and make new ones, she's going to discover that her unique perspective on people might lead her into a deadly scenario.

General Montgomery has what he believes to be a solid plan. It's his destiny to save what's left of the people of the United States and he's willing to do whatever it takes to carry it out. He's learning that not everyone serving with him agrees, and The Man in the Mountain is starting to wage a new war.

Master Sergeant James Campbell is one of the weapons to be deployed, but the sergeant has his own secrets. When James finds himself on a convergence course with some important players, his 1st Force Recon Unit will play a pivotal role in the future of mankind.

Russell Boyd doesn't care about mankind, or even his own survival. It's all rather irrelevant to the universe. Because that's what really makes the decisions in the end: the universe. And he's simply an extension of it.

CHAPTER 1

TECHNICAL SERGEANT BEN OWEN
Near Flagstaff, Arizona

THE MOON CAST a pale light across the darkened landscape, providing just enough detail for Sergeant Ben Owen as he crept between the trees. His rapid, ragged breath came in short gasps so that it was all he could hear. Muscles burning from the exertion, Ben ignored the pain and focused on the task at hand.

FEMA Shelter AZ1 was large in comparison to some of the others, though at the moment the occupants were all military. In spite of it being one in the morning, the camp hummed with activity and Ben could see personnel moving about below him in numerous locations. That was good.

The sergeant swung his M-24 rifle around to the ready as he reached the position he'd scoped out earlier in the day. It was a low ridge located approximately five hundred feet from the camp, with an elevation of a hundred feet, give or take a few.

While no shot was ever easy, as a certified counter sniper in Afghanistan, Sergeant Owen had successfully completed much more difficult…missions.

That's what General Montgomery had called it when he'd pulled Ben aside before boarding the Huey as an escort for Admiral Baker; a mission.

Rapid gunfire erupted to the south of his location, and instead of reacting to it, he took a slow, steadying breath. The northern lights flickered above them all, casting its mystical illumination in with the dancing shadows of soldiers as they scurried about. From his vantage point, Ben could see what had already been reported: a large contingent of troops moving in from the south and another, smaller one from the north. Though impressive, they didn't stand a chance. It would be a bloodbath.

The reason given for sending Vice Admiral Baker to FEMA Shelter AZ1 was increasing reports of a planned attack by local militia. Unlike some of the other groups, these mercenaries were comprised of not only local civilians, but also law enforcement and some National Guard troops who had grown wary of their own military leaders. The admiral arrived under the guise of an emissary, as an attempt to thwart any continued violence and try to bring some resolution between the groups.

However, Ben had worked under General Montgomery for five years, so he wasn't surprised to discover an ulterior motive. That it would involve the assassination of the admiral *was* a shock, but Ben was a solider and he believed in his command. He'd seen firsthand, in the streets of Colorado Springs, what desperation and fear drove people to. It was worse than what he'd witnessed overseas, and he knew it would only get worse.

A blinding explosion exposed the scene below him in stark contrast, and Ben turned his head away from his scope, blinking rapidly to clear his vision. It looked like an M67 grenade, standard military issue, and would mark the beginning of an all-out assault attempt against the shelter.

Gunfire answered the detonation and there were shouts from near the back of the camp, where Ben was focusing his attention. That was the location of the Operations Command Center, where Admiral Baker was. As luck would have it, while Ben repositioned himself and did his best to ignore the increasing gunfight, the admiral emerged from the tent, a deep scowl on his face.

Time slowed down and his hearing receded as a massive surge of adrenaline coursed through Sergeant Owen's body. In that moment, he contemplated what he was about to do. If the truth were ever exposed, some would see it as a soldier following orders and playing a pivotal role in an attempt to save what was left of humanity. Others would call it the act of a traitor and a coward, cold-blooded murder carried out by the follower of a power-hungry lunatic.

On some level, Ben admitted that he thought he'd have more time to evaluate the situation and his role. They'd only arrived at the shelter twelve hours ago, but as fate would have it, it was on the eve of the very assault the admiral thought he had a chance to diplomatically prevent. Instead, he would end up a martyr for the very cause he was against, and the general could claim the admiral's death at the hands of the militia as a means to shut down the governor trying to force power back into the civilian government.

The northern lights flared momentarily, enveloping the wooded vista in a blanket of green and adding another layer of confusion and chaos to the pandemonium. Ben blinked once as his thoughts raced, shots echoed, and the lights merged, suspended in the moment.

Letting out his breath, the sergeant's body responded automatically to its training, his finger pulling back on the trigger as he confirmed the target was in his sights. Vice Admiral Baker began to fall before the report of the weapon was processed by Ben's brain, and he was already moving away as the only real tangible hope for the civilian government became nothing more than a notation in the history books.

CHAPTER 2

CHLOE
Miller Ranch, Mercy, Montana

CHLOE'S FEET beat out a rhythm on the trail and she hummed along with it under her breath, keeping cadence. Since listening to music while she jogged wasn't an option anymore, she had plenty of time to work on her singing voice.

The weather had done another one-eighty since the storm three days ago, and the morning started out hot and humid, with clear skies. Chloe wiped at the sweat beaded on her forehead, thankful again for her short hair. The purple was almost completely faded from the tips and she had started wearing a headband most days, which kept her overgrown bangs out of her eyes.

She was a mile in on the Miner's Trail, which was her favorite stretch so far. The cedar trees there were massive and created a sort of cathedral-like effect for a quarter mile before the path started its climb farther into the mountains. Looking up from her feet, she caught a glimpse of the steep and ragged highlands jutting up in the distance.

The musty smell of the earth mingled with warmed pine needles, creating an enticing aroma that would beckon to Chloe long after she left the trail. She found the exercise addictive, almost to the point of being obsessed with getting lost in the remote wilderness. There was something about the whisper of the wind in the trees, and the vast stretches of back country that made her feel…normal. Like her problems, or even the problems of the whole town, were small and inconsequential as long as she was in the expanse. It was cathartic and Chloe couldn't remember a time she'd ever felt so light and unburdened. Then, she'd get back into town and would be bombarded with the reality of what they were up against, and as the weight descended again, all she could think of was the need to get back into the mountains.

Chloe's foot caught on a root and she stumbled forward, flailing her arms briefly before she caught herself. She'd gotten pretty good at recovering from tripping up and had only taken a couple of falls in the past week. Deciding it was a good time to stop for a drink, Chloe glared back at the offending root as she unscrewed the top of her water bottle. Since she was out for a fairly short run, there wasn't any reason to bring a backpack or anything other than water. She preferred to travel light, in spite of Bishop's warnings against being out in the woods alone.

Strolling along, she neared the spot where the cedars thinned out and gave way to grasses and rocks. Chloe poured some water over her head in anticipation of the sun blazing down on her. It trickled through her hair and then down the front of her shirt, and she pulled at the fabric to help fan herself. She was rather proud of what she'd dubbed her "running shirt". It was tan, with an iconic picture of Luke Skywalker with Yoda on his back and the words "May The Force Be With You", emblazoned across the bottom. She'd cut the sleeves off to make it into a tank top, and thought it quite fitting.

Lingering in the shade of the trees, Chloe debated whether she should go another mile or just turn back. Sandy was already getting her horse saddled when she'd left, and would be in the upper pasture by then. The cattle had started calving, so it was important to make sure they had plenty of grass to graze on, and Chloe's favorite job was to walk through the tall meadows and check for any newborn calves hidden in the foliage. She'd had no idea baby cows were so darn cute.

Vacillating between the lure of the wilds and the knowledge that Sandy was waiting on her, Chloe squinted up at the craggy peaks. Maybe, if she simply soaked up the calming energy for a few minutes, it would be enough to get her through the rest of the day, and she could come back for an evening run. Having made up her mind, she began to turn away, but some unexpected movement in the distance caused her to freeze.

Thinking it must be an elk or maybe even a bear, Chloe crept forward to get a better view. Whatever it was, it looked like it was on the trail right before it disappeared over the first ridge and down into one of many smaller valleys. The top of that crest was the farthest Chloe had gotten in her explorations, and she knew it was about four miles from where she currently stood.

Frowning, she shrugged her shoulders against a prickling sensation that wound its way up her spine to settle at the base of her neck. That wasn't an animal. At least, not *only* an animal. As they made their way down the hillside, Chloe saw that it was, in fact, a horse and rider. A large rider dressed all in black, and he wasn't alone. Another horse began the descent, also with a man dressed in dark clothing. As a third horse emerged, Chloe spun around and began to run.

Her mind raced and her legs burned as she hurled herself recklessly down the trail, leaping over obstacles and counting on her surefootedness to not let her down. There'd been a growing concern over the safety of the herd and the obvious target they made for any number of groups. The altercation with Jason and his friends at the lake aside, the guards posted on the road had fended off their fair share of roaming, desperate people.

Chloe's heart surged painfully in her chest as she considered the all-black attire. It suggested an organized threat. She had to consider them dangerous until proven otherwise. That was the mentality Bishop had been hammering into them for the past two weeks. Based on the reports coming in, he was right in his approach.

Barely ducking in time to avoid a low-hanging branch, Chloe gasped and then tossed her water bottle aside. She'd need both of her hands free if she fell. The ranch was less than a mile away, and she knew Bishop would be at the far end of the nearest field, mending the last part of the fence that was destroyed in the storm.

Five minutes later, red-faced and gulping for air, Chloe staggered into the field, her legs threatening to collapse from under her. "Bishop!" she shouted, frustrated by how weak her voice sounded. "Bishop! Riders! Riders are coming!"

She could see him in the distance, an arm raised over his head, about to swing a hammer. Bishop paused and turned, staring at her for a moment before lifting both of his hands at her questioningly. He couldn't hear her.

Close to panic, Chloe began to wave her arms furiously at him as she forced her body to keep going. "Riders!" she screamed, her voice cracking as she stepped in a low spot and almost fell. Bishop dropped the hammer and started running. Whether he finally heard her or simply realized how frantic she was, it didn't really matter. He was moving.

They both got to the barn at the same time, and Chloe was surprised at the concern she saw on the older man's face. He clearly thought something had happened to her. She pointed back the way she'd come and swallowed once to gather her voice. "A couple miles back, now. There's a group of people on horses. They're dressed all in black."

"How many?"

The speed with which Bishop switched from concern to action was dizzying. Chloe followed as he sped into the barn and ran for the rifles. "Um, I'm not sure. I saw three, I think, but there could be more."

"Any weapons?" Bishop shouldered a rifle and then yanked the handheld radio off his belt.

"I didn't see any, but they were too far away to be sure."

Bishop spoke into the radio while grabbing the second rifle they always stored in the barn. "Sheriff Waters, this is Bishop, come in. We have an urgent situation."

"Give me the other rifle," Chloe demanded, holding out a hand. When Bishop frowned at her, she pursed her lips. "Don't look at me like that! I'm not going inside."

"Go get Sandy," he ordered before turning away from her, the other rifle still in his grasp.

"No!" Chloe snapped. She ignored the ache in her thighs as she pushed them to catch up to Bishop. He was already heading back outside. "They'll be here before I can reach her. Give me the gun!"

Bishop stopped just beyond the open doors of the barn and scowled at her. "The fact that you'd call it a gun and not a rifle is one of the reasons I'm not giving it to you."

Chloe's face burned red. "I know how to shoot!"

"Bishop, this is Waters. What sort of situation?"

"Got at least three riders coming down Miner's Trail. Dressed in black, unknown if armed." Bishop lowered the radio without waiting for a response, and clipped it back on to his belt as a large black-and-white horse galloped into the far side of the field. Its rider was equally large, and the way he handled the horse left no question as to his ability. He sported a beard, and dark hair stuck out from under a dirty and worn cowboy hat. Chloe could see a gun strapped to his right thigh, and Bishop must have seen it at the same time because he silently thrust the other rifle at her as another rider trotted into view.

Seizing the weapon, she clenched her teeth together, nostrils flaring. Miller Ranch had become her home and there wasn't anything she wouldn't do to protect it. It wasn't until that moment that Chloe realized how much she cared about Sandy, Bishop, and Crissy. They were her family.

"That's far enough!" Bishop growled, raising his rifle.

The man was about fifty feet away, and while he'd slowed his horse to a walk, he wasn't stopping. There was an air about him that even Chloe recognized as the same type of power Bishop possessed. Her breath caught in her throat as she realized it wasn't going to end well.

"Where's Sandy Miller?" the man demanded, his voice deep and booming. His eyes were wild, and he looked like a panther crouched and about to spring. There were fading bruises under both of his eyes, and a nasty-looking wound over his right eyebrow. In spite of his rough appearance and the distance between them, there was something about him that seemed familiar to Chloe. As he spoke, his hand lowered to the pistol at his thigh.

"I wouldn't do that," Bishop cautioned, making a point of pulling back the bolt action and slapping it into place. "Who are you?"

Two more horses came pounding into the field before any answers could be given, and Chloe's confusion grew as she saw it was a formidable woman and a teen boy. As he approached, she recognized the boy's features and everything fell into place.

Lowering the rifle, she raised her free hand toward Bishop and motioned for him to do the same.

"Stop!" All six of them turned as one to look toward Sandy as she came galloping down the hill on her mount, hair loose and flying behind her. "It's my son!" she screamed, sounding almost hysterical. "Thomas!"

Her smile spreading as Bishop lowered his weapon, Chloe turned back to look again at the ragtag group coming closer. The large man was already off his horse and running toward Sandy, and the boy she now knew was Ethan pulled to a stop right in front of her. He leapt down from the horse to follow his dad, but paused when he saw Chloe. His face scrunched up in a pained expression as he turned back to her. "What'd ya do to my shirt?"

CHAPTER 3

*T*OM

Miller Ranch, Mercy, Montana

TOM'S FEET barely hit the ground before his mom leapt from her horse and slammed into him. "Is it really you?" she cried into his chest, her voice muffled by his shirt. He wrapped his arms around her and held on tight, afraid to let go. After eighteen days of struggling to reach her, now that they were home it didn't seem real.

Leaning back, Sandy reached up and cradled his face in her hands, searching his eyes. "Oh, my poor Tom," she gasped, tracing a finger over his eye and along the wound on his forehead. "What happened to you?"

"Grandma?" Sandy dropped one hand and pivoted to pull Ethan into the embrace, saving Tom from having to answer her question. It was a good thing, too, because he didn't trust his voice.

"I knew you'd come home to me," Sandy sobbed, holding them both.

Tom rested his chin on the top of her head, the way he'd always done since he was tall enough, her black hair blowing in his face. As he did so, he glanced over at the older man standing awkwardly with the rifle still in his hand. "Are you okay, Mom?" he asked, his voice shaky.

Grasping each of their arms, Sandy took a step back and nodded at the man and young girl next to him. "This is Bishop and Chloe. They're the reason I've been okay, Tom. They've helped keep the farm going."

"Crissy!" the girl named Chloe shouted while rushing to meet a young blonde girl running through the field. She was holding a chicken.

"I heard the yelling!" Crissy said, looking at them all fearfully. "Are you okay?"

"It's all right," Sandy reassured her. Tom must have looked as perplexed as he felt, because his mom laughed at him. "They were part of a hiking group led by Bishop when the event happened," she explained.

"How did you all end up here?" Danny asked, speaking for the first time. Tom turned to her and Sam, feeling overwhelmed.

"It's a long story," Bishop answered, shouldering the rifle and standing stiffly.

"We should all go inside and get acquainted," Sandy suggested, reaching out to take Tom's hand again, like she couldn't stand to let him get too far from her. "I can only imagine what you've all been through!" Kneeling down, she held her other hand out to Grace, who immediately began to lick her. "Oh, we're going to be *great* friends, aren't we?" she cooed.

Tom finally allowed himself to relax enough to introduce Sam and Danny. He was slowly getting over his initial reaction to shoot Bishop, except that he was a quiet man and that made Tom wary. He'd met too many people like that recently.

"Bishop, would you please take these horses and give them the royal treatment?" Sandy asked, gesturing for Danny and Sam to join them as they headed for the house. Tom noted Ethan was suddenly much more civilized and talkative as the two girls gravitated to him.

While it was an odd experience for Tom to feel like an intruder in his own home, he knew he needed to tread lightly. Fewer than three weeks had passed since the event, but it may as well have been a lifetime. They'd all changed, and he didn't know what his mother had been through during his absence.

As Sandy led the way into the house, Tom absorbed all of the familiar surroundings. He could literally feel the wariness and pain of the past few weeks seeping from his body, replaced with the love and comfort that Miller Ranch offered him.

"I'll admit to getting irritated with Patty more than once," Sandy was saying while gathering everyone into the family room. His mom had naturally started to tell her story first, including what had been happening in Mercy. She hadn't gotten very far, but it was already an interesting tale that involved a fair amount of politics. "The truth of it is that she's been in an impossible situation and has done her best. Not without some mistakes, but it's hard to blame her. I know you're likely to be unhappy with the plans to continue slaughtering cattle to feed the town—"

"No," Tom interrupted his mom. She seemed surprised. "I figured that would happen," he explained. "I'll sit down with Mayor Patty and this group of town leaders she's put together and have an honest discussion. I'm fine with giving whatever is needed to the town, but only if it's approached as a partnership. We need to have complete authority over when and how much we give, and so will the other ranchers in Mercy. So long as Miller Ranch is involved, nothing will ever be taken by force.

We've seen up close what that looks like," Tom added, looking over at Sam and Danny, who sat in the other two armchairs in the room.

"It's a fine line between doing what's best for everyone, and having it come at the cost of another's freedom or goodwill," Sam said solemnly. "In our situation, it's easy to justify theft or violence, but if we want Mercy to succeed long-term, it needs to be done right from the beginning. That means everyone working together willingly."

Sandy was nodding and she looked relieved as she smiled up at Tom. "I knew you'd help put this all into perspective," she said to him, close to tears. "People will listen to you, Tom. They always have."

Danny cleared her throat and Tom realized how thoughtless he was being. He jumped up before she could say anything. "We need to get you home," he said, reaching out a hand to pull her to her feet. "We can catch up on the rest when I get back," he said, turning to his mom.

"You don't have to go," Danny insisted after accepting his hand and standing wearily. She looked tired and emotionally drained. Now that they'd made it to Mercy, they were all exhausted. After being in fight-or-flight mode for so long, they had some serious sleep to catch up on.

"You already said you aren't sure how to get to your dad's from here," Tom said, though he could easily draw her a map. There was another reason he wanted to take her, and it had nothing to do with being a gentleman. Somewhere along the way, Tom had begun to feel protective of Danny and he wasn't ready to say goodbye.

"I can take them," the girl named Chloe offered. She and Crissy sat behind them, in the kitchen. "I've been to Tane's a couple of times." Danny raised her eyebrows at the girl, clearly surprised that she'd know her dad.

"Your father has been a huge help," Sandy explained. "He and Bishop are good friends, actually. And he isn't home right now. He'll be out at the spring, working on restoring the water supply after our last…mishap."

"Working?" Danny said incredulously. Her brows drew together in concern and Grace, who'd been lying contentedly in front of the cold fireplace, looked up at her and whined. "My dad has a heart condition. He shouldn't be out running around or doing anything strenuous. You need to take me to him," she ordered Chloe as she moved toward the backdoor.

Grace leapt to her feet and plodded after Danny, not waiting to be called, and Sam slowly followed. "I may as well tag along," he said with a wink to Ethan. "With any luck, we'll all sit down to a steak dinner soon."

Chloe rose from the stool at the kitchen counter and stopped Danny and Sam at the door. "I'm happy to take you, but I don't think we should go to the spring." The young girl looked meaningfully at Sandy. "We need to use the back roads and go straight to his house. They can wait for him there. If anyone sees them—"

Sandy cringed and put a hand to her forehead. "The quarantine!" Turning to Tom, she appeared apologetic. "After an outbreak of a horrible bacteria killed several people, we've had a strict quarantine protocol."

Danny's shoulders sagged. "Yeah, we've heard of it."

Tom shook his head at his mom's questioning look. "I'll explain later. It's a very long story."

The back door slid open with a flourish then and Bishop plodded inside, not bothering to shake off his boots and leaving a trail of dirt in his haste. The sound of approaching horses could be heard through the open door. "I radioed the sheriff and told him we were okay, but they've come anyway," he explained, gesturing with his hat to the front door. "You might want to preempt the introductions, Sandy. I'm not sure how clear they are on who's here, and why."

Tom followed his mom out onto the front porch and tried not to sigh when he saw the group of riders in the driveway. All he wanted was one day to decompress and regroup, but they seemed destined to always have some sort of conflict to resolve.

"Patty!" Sandy hollered, walking down the steps ahead of Tom. She waved at him to stay put as she approached the horses.

Tom watched as Mayor Patty slid off her horse but remained several feet away from his mom while eying him cautiously. He recognized her husband, Caleb, on the horse next to her. The sheriff, one of his deputies, and another man Tom wasn't familiar with fanned out to either side, making a formidable wall. Bishop moved up next to Tom, and he noticed how rigidly he stood, as if ready to move into action at any given moment. It wasn't the stance of an ordinary man.

"Praise the Lord, it's true!" Patty said, clapping her hands together once. "Your mom never gave up hope," she said to Tom, her expression still wary.

"Who else is with you?" Sheriff Waters asked bluntly. "You said there were several riders," he said to Bishop.

"Sheriff," Tom said, addressing the man formally. "My son, Ethan, is with me, as well as another man and woman we met along the way. Danny Latu and Sam Ruiz, a paramedic and teacher from Helena."

"Latu," Patty said thoughtfully. "Are you Tane's daughter?"

Tom turned to see that Danny had joined them on the porch, and she was nodding at Patty. "Yes. And I'd really like to see him."

"I'm afraid we'll have to ask you to postpone your reunion for another day," Sheriff Waters said gravely. "You've already avoided our normal protocol by coming in on the trail, and we can't have you wandering around town. It'll cause a panic."

Danny's face reddened and Tom was worried she'd lose her

temper, but she made an obvious effort to be reasonable. "Right. I get it. How about you tell him I'm here, then, and he can come out to see me?"

Patty frowned disapprovingly. "I'm sorry, but that isn't an option. Tane is a vital member of the team working at the spring and we can't afford to lose him right now. Bishop and Chloe were supposed to go help this afternoon, so now we're already going to be down two more people."

Danny's hands balled into fists and she stomped across the porch. "You have no right to keep me from my father!" she shouted.

Tom put a hand out to stop Danny when he saw the deputy and other man begin to reach for their sidearms. He didn't think they'd actually shoot her, but he'd had enough showdowns lately to last a lifetime. "Danny," he whispered gruffly. "This won't help you. We'll figure it out on our own."

To his relief, Danny didn't pull away from him. Although she was upset, she still had the ability to stop her emotional response and clearly evaluate the situation. He heard her take an audible breath before moving back a step and relaxing her hands.

"I have over a dozen fresh graves that work as a strong reminder why we can't place any more lives at risk," Patty tried to explain to them. "And while I understand that you just got here and can't fully appreciate the precarious situation we're in with our water supply, you have to trust me when I say that moving your reunion with your father up a day isn't worth the water we'd lose."

"She's right," Caleb said, his deep voice adding weight to the assertion. "You have no idea how relieved we are to have you home, Tom, and I can't wait to sit down and have a beer with you, but right now we've got to put the safety of Mercy first."

"We understand," Tom said, looking at Danny, and he was relieved when she nodded in agreement. "Maybe we can help."

When Patty and the sheriff regarded him silently, he continued. "How about, if we don't show any signs of infection after twelve hours, you notify Tane that we're here at the ranch? You can do it after they're done working for the day. Then he can join us for the night, if he wants to. Tomorrow, after we're cleared in the morning, we'll all go and work on the water. With the four of us helping, maybe we can make a difference."

Patty smiled sincerely for the first time and the other men with her all noticeably relaxed. "I think that's a great idea," she said. "I'll tell Tane myself, Danny. I promise."

Danny gave a small grin to the mayor and then sat resolutely in one of the chairs on the porch. Grace was instantly at her feet, tongue lolling, and she absently stroked the retriever's head as Sam came out and sat in the other chair.

Tom noticed that Ethan was standing in the doorway with Chloe and Crissy, taking the scene in. It wasn't exactly the homecoming they'd envisioned, but at least his mom was healthy and, compared to every other town they'd been to, Mercy was doing rather well, whether they realized it or not.

"How about you and Caleb come back tomorrow night?" Sandy suggested. "You too, Sheriff. We'll all have dinner together and get caught up on what's happening. I think Tom and his companions have a lot of useful information for us."

"I'd be very interested in hearing what you've encountered since the flashpoint," Sheriff Waters said.

Sam stood from his chair and moved to the front railing, looking down questioningly at the sheriff. "I'm curious, how do you know that the military is calling the event 'flashpoint'?"

"I was able to get my shortwave working the day it happened," Caleb answered. "It took some time, but I eventually managed to communicate with several operators around the world."

"You've been in contact with the military?" Tom asked,

alarmed. He exchanged a knowing look with both Danny and Sam, his anxiety ratcheting up.

"Not…recently," Patty said, hesitating. "We, um…" She looked at the sheriff, who gave a silent bob of his head before she continued. "Caleb *was* speaking with some military posts in a couple of states, until we led them to believe that we never managed to contain the cholera-like illness."

"Why would you do that?" Sandy asked. It was clear to Tom that it was the first his mom had heard of the deception.

"We started getting reports of forced FEMA camps and violent take-overs by the military," Sheriff Waters answered.

"So, you decided on behalf of the town to cut us off from any possible outside aid?" Sandy yelled, shocked. "What if they could have been helping us this whole time?"

"It was the right thing to do," Tom said, surprising both the sheriff and his mom. "At least, for now I think it is. Until the military and what's left of our government get a better grip on things, we're better off on our own."

"So it's true?" Patty asked, her face a picture of distress even though Tom had agreed with her. "Our Pony Express riders have been bringing back unbelievable stories of farmers being forced off their own land, and killed if they resist."

"It's true," Sam confirmed. "We've experienced it ourselves."

"Did you say Pony Express?" Danny stood and moved up next to Tom, her eyes wide.

"That's what we've been calling our system of riders," Caleb said, not understanding Danny's reaction. "It began as a mail service. We had them wearing the Mercy post office shirts until we realized it wasn't smart to advertise where our home base was. It's already expanded into a large network connecting several communities. We've started a supply chain and are trying to accommodate as many people as possible."

"Are you missing any riders?" Tom asked, afraid he already knew the answer.

Patty glanced sideways at the sheriff. "Yes," Sheriff Waters confirmed. "Two. They're overdue going on three days now."

"We know where they are," Danny said, hanging her head as she recalled the scene.

Tom set a hand over top of hers on the railing. "The military isn't the only threat out there," he said grimly. "And if these guys know about Mercy, we'd better get ready. They'll be coming."

CHAPTER 4

GENERAL MONTGOMERY
Cheyenne Mountain, Colorado

GENERAL MONTGOMERY'S office door flew open and Colonel Walsh barged in unannounced. He gripped a sheet of paper and his face was ashen. "We've just gotten confirmation that an assault was successfully launched against FEMA Shelter AZ1 early this morning," Walsh blurted before setting the report down on Montgomery's desk.

He glanced down at the memo and noted the familiar handwritten words. Their shortwave radio operator was good at what he did, but his penmanship left a lot to be desired. Pushing it aside, he preferred to get it directly from Walsh. "While we weren't expecting them to move this soon, it's not as if it's a surprise." Though he outwardly remained unfazed by the news, Montgomery was silently relieved that they'd managed to get the admiral there in time. He had faith that Sergeant Owen successfully completed his mission. He wasn't the kind of soldier to accept failure.

"Of course we knew something was being planned," Walsh confirmed, frowning. "Except it was very coordinated. That was in part due to the insurgents being made up of more than just local civilians. We've got good intel that it was led by some police officers and even state guardsmen. As a result, we took more casualties than anticipated in the attack."

"You mean the terrorist attack."

"Sir?"

Montgomery rested his hands on the top of his desk and leaned forward while leveling a stony gaze at Walsh. "From now on, any communication regarding this incident will refer to it as a *terrorist* attack. Are we clear?"

"But, sir—"

"Is there a problem, Colonel?" Montgomery growled, his voice getting dangerously loud.

"No, sir." Walsh cleared his throat, obviously uncomfortable with the conversation. "It's just that some of those men and women involved in the confron—I mean, terrorist attack, were locals. And the National Guard members live in the area, too. People aren't going to blindly accept that they're terrorists simply because we say so."

General Montgomery rose halfway from his leather office chair before slamming his fists down, causing Walsh to jump back. "We've gone from a world of instant, constant data exchange, to one where only a handful of people can communicate by tapping out a code!" he spat. "*We* now control the information both coming and going. It's never been easier to shape our own reality and because of this, I fully expect the world to believe those terrorists are whoever we say they are."

"Yes, sir," Walsh mumbled, shaken. "I'll go speak with our communications center personally."

"I can't stress enough how critical this is," the general insisted, stopping Walsh from turning away from him. "You know why this battle has to be depicted correctly. Right, Colonel? Admiral Baker must be made into a martyr. Only then can we make it the military's mission to avenge his death, and close the book on any possible civilian government. Not even the remaining governors or senators can support blatant anarchy."

Walsh tipped his head questioningly, his face suddenly becoming stoic. "That was my next report, sir. That Vice Admiral Baker might be one of the casualties. It hasn't been confirmed yet."

General Montgomery swallowed hard, his face unflinching. The clock ticked from its perch on the wall, confirming the number of seconds the silence stretched as the two men stared at each other across the desk.

"That will be all, Colonel," Montgomery finally ordered, not feeling the need to justify himself to anyone, not even Walsh. It was better that way.

The colonel hesitated, his eyes narrowing for only a moment as he absorbed the meaning of the exchange and the fact that he wasn't going to be given an explanation for it. In the end, he did what Montgomery knew he would do; he turned around and walked away to carry out his commander's orders.

The general allowed him to get as far as the door. "Kelly."

The other man stopped with his hand on the doorknob, frozen by the rare use of his first name.

"Do you trust me?" Montgomery meant to sound confident and strong in his resolve, but it instead came out as a plea to his longtime friend.

Walsh's shoulders sagged but he didn't turn around. "I want to."

General Montgomery sat rigidly and watched as the colonel walked through the door without another word.

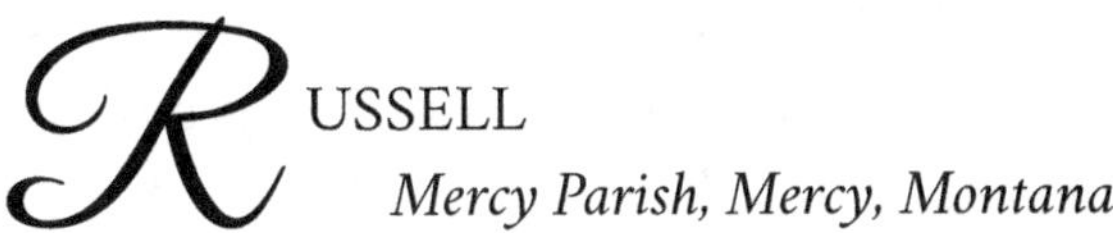

CHAPTER 5

RUSSELL
Mercy Parish, Mercy, Montana

RUSSELL PULLED on the large rope with all of his strength, while marveling at how the late Father White had managed to do it. An ear-splitting clanging surrounded him when he succeeded in his task, and he clenched his teeth as he made sure to ring the church bell the allotted number of times.

Madeline had made it very clear that to summon the congregation, he was to toll the bell seven times, a half-hour before the service. The pianist was proving to be of great assistance. Russell didn't even know it was going to be Sunday until the night before. She had shown up on his doorstep, still tearful over the news of the passing of her beloved Pastor White.

Happy to invite the friendly woman in, they sat for over an hour discussing exactly how the Father had performed his Sunday mass, to be certain Russell honored his memory. Well, that was the guise he used to refresh his recollection on how the proceedings should be performed.

Thankfully, the memorial service for the pastor wouldn't be for another three days, though they buried him right away. Madeline insisted she needed the time to prepare a proper commemorative celebration in his honor, and wanted to make sure there was plenty of notice for the community to attend.

Russell slowly made his way down the steep, rickety wooden steps of the bell tower, delaying the inevitable. He could hear people already moving about in the church below him. According to Madeline, they were eager to meet their new, young priest.

The staircase led directly into his office, where Russell stood debating whether to wear the traditional robes or not. While it might give him an additional air of authority in the eyes of his congregation, the fact remained that he wasn't Catholic, nor had he ever pretended to be. Donning the sacred clothing could be taking his role too far, and one thing Russell comprehended was how important it was to recognize certain limitations. Staying within them while still manipulating everything else around him was how he tended to get whatever he wanted.

A short time later, after the appropriate hymns had been played, he walked out into the sanctuary still dressed in his humble street clothes. Raising his hands to silence the crowd, he stood there for a moment in the pregnant pause, milking it as much as possible. Finally, Russell slowly brought his hands together and peered out at the congregation over his fingertips.

"To my brothers and sisters of Sanctuary, I want to thank you for welcoming me into your home and church. My name is Father Russell Rogers, and I have traveled here...no, I was *led* here from a great distance. There are no coincidences when it comes to the plans of the universe." Russell knew how his smooth voice and refined look affected people, and when put into a position of power, it was as dangerous as any weapon. The small nods, quick exchanges of approving looks, and beguiled smiles returned to him were all signs of how his spell was already successfully cast. And he'd only just begun.

"Although I have so much more I want to share with you, I feel strongly that this is not my time to say it. You have all suffered yet another great loss in a string of many, and in honor of Father White, I'm dedicating this service to him and his memory. For that reason, in lieu of a sermon, I'm going to ask Madeline to step out from behind her piano and speak about the man you all loved so dearly."

Madeline stood with a shocked expression, a hand flying to her throat in what Russell now realized was her frequent gesture of surprise. Blushing furiously, she rushed to make her way around the piano, her skirt snagging on an edge in the process. Russell stifled a snort as the churchgoers barely avoided more revelations than expected that Sunday.

The expose averted, Madeline enthusiastically spoke of the late priest and his work. As her voiced droned on, Russell was happy to take a seat and block it all out. His mind drifted to the work he was to do that afternoon at the clinic with the lovely Dr. Melissa Olsen. She had invited him to dinner later that week and he was tempted to accept, even though there was no guarantee he'd still be around.

Through his charity work over the past few days, Russell had come to learn just how desperate the water situation was in Mercy. If the leaders had been less concerned about politics, they might have foreseen other issues more clearly. He sighed. It was always the same. Even with a life-altering event, in a small and genuine community like Mercy, the basis of human nature still prevailed. They were lucky he'd arrived when he did.

"Father?"

Russell jerked to attention and looked up to find Madeline staring at him earnestly.

"Father, would you like to close the service?" Her hand at her throat again, Madeline offered him a small smile before returning to her post at the piano.

Standing, Russell reflected on the people seated at his back. His flock, desperate for leadership. Unfortunately for them, he'd be moving on soon. He still had a lot of work to be done outside of Mercy, now that he understood they were to succumb to the same natural consequences as everyone else. Although sometimes nature needed a helping hand.

Turning, Russell raised his hands with a flourish. "Let us pray!"

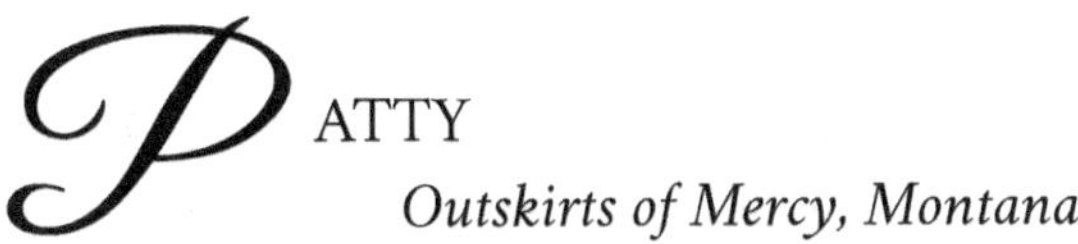

CHAPTER 6

ATTY

Outskirts of Mercy, Montana

THE SUN WAS ALREADY at her back as Patty rode along the familiar country road on the outskirts of Mercy. She'd just left the spring, where she had the pleasure of telling Tane that his daughter was waiting to see him at Miller Ranch. Patty smiled, recalling the expression on the large man's face. It was a joy most of them didn't get to experience lately...the reunion with a loved one once thought lost.

Patty was weary after another emotional day and was more than ready to go home, but she had an important stop to make first. Her friend, Kathy, lived by herself and was only a couple of miles out of the way. Though physically active and more than five years younger than Patty, Kathy had recently been diagnosed with an aggressive type of cancer and had undergone her second round of chemotherapy a few days before the flashpoint. Her immune system already weakened, the gamma radiation had nearly killed her, in the cruelest twist of irony. To Melissa's utter shock, her patient not only survived, but was defying all logic and getting *better*.

Patty simply chose to call it a miracle. With so many stories of loss and horror, Kathy's was one that she clung to. It reminded her that the will to live was as equally important as the opportunity. Even though Kathy had every reason to give up, including the fact that her remaining family had died on the East Coast, she chose instead to smile through her misery and come out the other side.

Urging her horse into a trot down the length of Kathy's long driveway, Patty soaked up the nostalgic scene. The late afternoon sunlight cast warm shadows through the evergreens that lined the gravel road and birds flitted amongst them, chirping as she passed underneath. It was enough to allow Patty a moment of respite, where she could imagine it was the same as any other day she'd gone for a ride to have afternoon tea with her friend. Before they lost so much, but also gained so much insight.

"Patty!"

Patty held a hand up to shield her eyes, and saw that Kathy had come down from her front porch to greet her. She looked good. Reining her horse in, she jumped down and waved a greeting before lifting the bundle down from the back of her saddle. Inside was an assortment of apples, corn, potatoes, and beef jerky. Kathy was one of the lucky few who had a hand pump attached to her well, so she was set for water.

"What a wonderful surprise," Kathy said as she rushed to give Patty a hug. "Oh, you shouldn't have," she lamented when Patty held the bag out.

"Of course I should have," Patty retorted playfully. "There's a couple of teabags in there, too. The good stuff," she winked, eliciting gentle laughter from the other woman. "Your color is remarkably good."

Kathy nodded and raised a hand to her cheek after hefting the bag under her other arm. "I don't know what it is, Patty, but I feel better than I have in months. I was already planning on going into town tomorrow to help at the farmer's market you've been going on about."

Patty beamed at her friend, unable to contain her excitement. "It'll be so great to have you there! I'll be arriving around mid-morning, after I get caught up on some paperwork at city hall."

"Perfect." Kathy opened the front door and then looked back expectantly at Patty. "You're coming in, aren't you? I'll make us some of that tea."

Patty's grin faded slightly and she wavered, tempted by the offer. "I wish I could. I really do, but I'm already late getting home. Caleb is still another hour behind me, so if I don't get going, we won't be eating dinner tonight."

Instead of being persistent, Kathy gave her an understanding look and patted the bag under her arm. "Well, then I'll have to enjoy it by myself, this one time. I fully expect you to come by tomorrow after the market and spend some time chatting with me though. I miss our talks."

Patty rushed up the front steps and gave Kathy a quick hug, thankful to have someone in her life who could offer some balance to all the craziness. "Absolutely!"

Trotting back down the driveway, the contrast of the trees seemed harsher and the air cooler, as she headed back into her role as mayor, healer, and wife. Patty felt pulled in so many directions that she wasn't sure what hat she truly wore anymore.

A mile down the road, she studied a small cabin set back in the woods, and had to squint at the sunlight reflecting off the windows. She believed a young man named Joseph currently lived there. Patty didn't know much about him except that he'd been a long-haul driver who rented the place cheap so he could crash there on the days he wasn't out on the road. Slowing, she wondered where his semi was, and assumed he must have been driving somewhere close by when the gamma ray struck.

Frowning, Patty considered whether to pay the man a quick visit. She'd seen him going into the only bar, The Last Stop, early the day before. While at the spring, she was told he'd never shown up for his shift that morning. It infuriated her that a young, able-bodied man had the energy to go into town to drink but not to pitch in and help out where he was needed.

Her good mood already precarious, Patty decided to let it go and have Caleb talk to him the next day instead. However, as she started back down the road, Joseph's horse came trotting around the side of his house and halfway out to where she was.

"You've got to be kidding me," Patty muttered, turning around. It was bad enough that he wasn't pulling his weight in town, but he couldn't even take care of his own animal?

Fortunately, the mare wasn't skittish, and she stood quietly as Patty took ahold of the bridle and led her around the cabin. She had no idea where the gate to the pasture was, but figured it was back behind the house somewhere. She would put the horse out in the field and then give Joseph an earful.

The side yard was badly overgrown and was likely that way long before the power went out. Garbage was piled up alongside the house, and Patty grimaced at the smell and batted flies away as she walked past. Most people had taken to either burning or burying their garbage. Leaving it out like that would only lead to a rodent problem, or even lure a bear into the neighborhood.

Her list of complaints growing, Patty's steps picked up steam along with her indignation. By the time she rounded the corner and found his body, her face was burning with anger. The heat in her cheeks rapidly faded, as well as the color, and Patty's hand fell from the bridle to clasp instead at her chest.

No more than twenty feet away, Joseph lay prone alongside a woodshed. His rifle was partway under his body and still clasped in his left hand. He'd shot himself in the head, and from the looks of it, had done a proper job.

A small gasp escaped Patty's lips as a torrent of emotions welled up inside of her. She'd seen plenty of death, both as a nurse and more recently as mayor. That wasn't what stole her breath and made her blood run cold. It was the knowledge that Joseph, a strong and able man of barely thirty, had lost so much hope that he'd been driven to take his own life.

There was a note in the dirt by his foot, but it was splattered with blood and she couldn't bring herself to pick it up. Probably best to leave it for the sheriff, anyway. Thinking about the ride back into town caused another emotion to override the rest: shame.

Dropping to her knees, Patty looked away from the once-handsome man, and instead focused on the late-afternoon light in the field. Insects danced in the hazy glare and the silence was so complete that she could hear her heartbeat. It reminded Patty that she was still alive, and that perhaps she'd lost some of her focus amongst all the concern of what others were thinking of her decisions as mayor.

A sob escaped her then, and Patty nearly choked on the realization that she'd failed Joseph. "I'm sorry," she whispered into the silence. She felt no resentment toward the young man, only sorrow.

Forcing herself to look at him, Patty sucked in a ragged breath. "I'm sorry I didn't come sooner, Joseph. I'm sorry I didn't ask you why you never came to the barbeques. I noticed that you always walked with your head down, and were drinking alone in the middle of the day, but I never cared enough to wonder *why*."

Slowly, Patty staggered to her feet and reached back blindly for the horse that was still there, waiting patiently. She thought of her friend Kathy. Alone in the world and dying of cancer, she managed to find the strength to not only live, but love life, while a young man with so much potential gave up.

"Hope," Patty sighed, determined his death would not be in vain. "I've forgotten that we need so much more than water and food." Uncertain as to how she could reach those in despair, Patty knew that she'd have to start by being honest with the community. Gary had been right in that respect, at least. She'd make an announcement assuring that everyone in Mercy would be given food and water, whether they chose to participate in the exchange or not. Tom Miller would be the perfect spokesperson to spread the word. He was the most respected rancher in Mercy, and people would listen to him.

Heading back to her own horse with the mare in tow, Patty paused at the edge of the yard and looked back at Joseph, his body already claimed by shadows. "I'm sorry you died alone."

CHAPTER 7

THAN
Miller Ranch, Mercy, Montana

DINNER WAS an interesting mix of fulfillment and misery. Ethan had been fantasizing about a good steak more than he'd care to admit, and while the roasted chicken wasn't quite as satisfying, it was a close second. On the other hand, the nonstop conversation between nine people was overwhelming, not to mention the questions his grandma kept asking him. At least Tane was the only extra body there that night, since the sheriff and mayor didn't want to risk exposing themselves by accepting the invitation to dinner.

When the adults retired to the campfire to sing Kumbaya and drink beers, Ethan saw his chance to escape. Especially since his dad refused to allow the teens to have any alcohol, even though it was literally the end of the world. He happily offered to help Chloe move out of his room when she announced she was on her way to go get her things. He had mixed feelings when he found out that while Crissy had been living in the guest room, and Bishop was in his dad's, the cute but abrasive girl had been assigned his bedroom.

Sleeping in his own bed was the other thing Ethan had been dreaming about, and he wasn't sure if he was irritated or thrilled that Chloe had been using it for practically the whole time. As he leaned against the doorframe and watched her stuff her clothes into a bag, he realized that most of the items were *his* that she had hijacked. Okay…irritated. He was definitely leaning more towards irritated.

One of Chloe's gifts must have been mind reading, because she looked up then and offered him a lopsided grin. "Sorry. Your grandma said this was all mostly stuff that was too small for you now."

"Yeah, most of it," Ethan agreed, maintaining his casual pose. "But *Star Wars?*" he asked, pointing at the altered tank sitting out on the bed.

Chloe grimaced. "Yeah, well…I know it's like, bordering on sacrilegious, but it was too big and Yoda is my favorite."

Ethan snorted. "Favorite? What, you're gonna claim to be a fan after destroying that vintage tee?"

"It's vintage?" Chloe sounded horrified.

It was his turn to grin. "Nah, I got it off Amazon for ten bucks. But it could have been!"

Chloe chuckled and looked impressed, rather than annoyed by the joke. "And yes, I'm a self-proclaimed nerd. Though, while Yoda is my favorite character, *Firefly* is my all-time favorite show."

Nodding in approval, Ethan pushed away from the door and entered his room. "Agreed." Maybe she wasn't so bad, after all.

She watched him as he plopped down in a beanbag and

propped his feet up on the bed next to where she was sitting. "BSG is a close second," she said once he was situated.

"*Battlestar Galactica*, the reboot?" Ethan asked, crinkling his nose. "No way. I never got into it."

Turning to face him, Chloe avoided his bare feet like they were a snake and continued to pack the last of her clothes while they talked. "It's one of the best storylines ever produced," she insisted. "How far did you get?"

"Never made it through season one."

"Well, that's why," Chloe said as if she'd just figured out some major mystery.

Ethan thought it was cute how animated she got talking about something as simple as a TV show. He assumed she was smart, so he was glad they shared something in common to talk about.

"You've got to watch it through at least the second season, and then I promise you won't be able to stop—" she froze mid-sentence, realizing what she was saying.

"The power will come back on," Ethan said softly. "Maybe not for a while, but it will, eventually."

"What if it doesn't?" Chloe asked matter-of-factly. "What if no one ever gets to watch any of those shows ever again?"

Of all the things in the world to mourn, it seemed ridiculous to be upset over the loss of some TV series. Yet, it was a sad reminder of how much they'd had ripped away. Chunks of their childhood, their culture, the simple pleasure of getting lost in an alternate reality where nothing else mattered for just a little while. The thought gave Ethan an idea and he tried to smile reassuringly at Chloe. "It's a good thing most of these stories were based on books!"

"True," she agreed, and then frowned again. "Except it's a little hard to get to your local library and request a copy."

Holding a finger up, Ethan jumped up and went to his closet. Opening it with a flourish, he opened one of the built-in cabinets inside and pulled out a plastic tub. He sat it on the bed with a small grunt and then lifted the lid off, revealing several dozen paperbacks.

Gasping in pleasure, Chloe got up on her knees and started digging through the books. "*Star Wars* and *Star Trek!*" she beamed, pulling several copies out. "How did I miss this?"

"You went through my stuff?" Ethan asked, his grin fading.

Laughing, Chloe reached out and pushed lightly against his chest. "Don't worry, I stayed out of your sock drawer. Any secrets hidden in there remain totally incognito."

Blushing, Ethan vacillated again on whether he liked the precocious teen or not. He'd never met anyone like her before. "Where's Crissy?" he asked, deciding it was best to change the subject altogether.

"Sleeping," Chloe sighed, sitting back on the bed with several books piled into her lap. "She's getting up at the crack of dawn to take care of the chickens so she can get into town and spend some time with Trevor."

"The other guy who was part of your hiking group?" Ethan asked, trying to remember the brief story Bishop had told them earlier in the day.

Chloe bobbed her head while making a pained expression. "He and Crissy are…close."

"That's a bad thing?"

The look Chloe gave him in response was hard to interpret, other than it wasn't a good topic. "No, not a bad thing, just irritating. He hurt his leg in that wagon accident Sandy told you about, and you'd think he was some hero with the way Crissy waits on him."

"You don't like him?" Ethan tried again. He didn't understand why, but a small part of him was put off that she might be jealous.

Huffing, Chloe added the books to her clothes and closed up the duffle bag. "He's my friend. They're both my friends, which is why I guess sometimes I feel a little like the third wheel. It wasn't like that until Crissy got all heartsick over him. What about you?" she asked bluntly. "You have a girlfriend back in Vegas?"

Thrown off by how quickly she'd flipped the conversation back to him, Ethan fumbled with his answer. "Me? Um, no. I mean, not at the time. Well, when I left for the summer, I didn't." His faced burned hotter when she laughed at his awkwardness, and he wondered if she was ever going to leave his room. "You and Crissy going to have enough space, sharing the room?" he asked, hoping she'd get the hint.

"More room than you and your dad will," she said, pointing at his full-size mattress. "Except that the other times we shared a bed, I usually woke up with Crissy's feet in my back. I'll let you know in the morning how it goes." Winking, she finally stood and headed for the door. "Where are Danny and her dad going to sleep tonight?"

Ethan shrugged. "I dunno. The couches, I guess. I think I heard Sam say they were all going to camp out there. Or my grandma probably has a couple of cots. I know Danny would sleep on the floor of the barn and not care."

Chloe paused, considering what he'd said. "She seems pretty cool. Tough, ya know? I guess she has to be if she's a firefighter."

"I watched her kill someone." Ethan didn't know why he said it. He hadn't planned to, and once it was out, he wished he could take it back. It was a statement that would lead to questions and he wasn't prepared to share any of the answers.

Chloe squinted at him, seemingly assessing the validity of his words. She must have seen something on his face that convinced her, because she simply sat her bag down and took over his previous position in the doorway. "How?"

"How?" Ethan echoed, unsure what she meant.

"How did she kill him? Like, slit his throat or—"

"She shot him," he interrupted. "In the chest. Then he fell off his horse. Well, partway; his foot was stuck in the stirrup, so it dragged him. By the time I got Tango stopped, Decker was dead. So, technically, I'm not sure if it was the bullet or horse that killed him."

Chloe stood staring at him, mouth open in a silent O. For the second time in as many minutes, Ethan had spoken without giving any thought to what he was saying. Maybe it was because he was home and now that some of his defenses were down, the stuff that was too hard to keep inside was oozing out, like a leak in a septic system. Closing his eyes and turning his head away from her judging eyes, Ethan wanted nothing more than to go to sleep and forget about everything.

"I'm sorry."

Ethan opened one eye and risked looking back at Chloe. To his surprise, she looked anguished instead of disapproving. Maybe, in time, he could tell her more about what he experienced, and it would help some of his nightmares go away.

"I'm glad she killed him, if he's one of the men that did that to you," she said, gesturing to his face and the bruises that hadn't completely faded. "He deserved it." Chloe's voice was harsh, and it had an edge to it that convinced Ethan she meant what she said.

As the short, attractive girl with purple in her hair walked away from Ethan's room, he felt like a small amount of the weight he'd been carrying around left with her. It was a little easier to breathe, and he was certain he'd have longer stretches of sleep in between his nightmares that night.

He didn't have a reasonable explanation for the connection he felt to Chloe, other than the fact she'd been sleeping in his room and going through his things for the past two weeks, but Ethan knew it was there. A familiarity, perhaps, of losing your parent and being cast into a situation you had no control over. Shaking his head and chastising himself for being overly emotional, Ethan got up and closed the door.

Going back to the bed, he saw that she'd left the *Star Wars* shirt behind. Grinning, he carefully draped it on the beanbag. Ethan had a feeling that when it came to Chloe, he'd need all the help from the Force he could get.

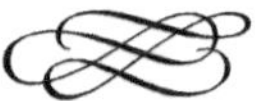

CHAPTER 8

ANNY
Miller Ranch, Mercy, Montana

DANNY HAD SPENT SO many nights sitting next to a campfire that it was the last thing she thought she'd choose to do on their first night in Mercy. However, when dinner was over and she had a chance to truly sit down with her dad and talk, doing it around a fire seemed fitting. It turned out that Sandy hadn't broken out Tom's reserve while he was gone, so they also had plenty of beer to toast with.

"You said you have a week of meds left?" she asked her dad as they picked seats next to each other. Grace plodded out onto the back patio with them, extremely content after a big bowl of chicken and carrots.

"Yes, Danny." He didn't roll his eyes at her, but Tane didn't need to. The tone of his voice said it all. It was one of the first questions she'd already asked him after their emotional reunion on the front porch less than an hour before. "I read you should have a month's worth of all your meds stored up, in case of a disaster. For once, I took some good advice."

Though he winked at her, Danny couldn't let it go. While she was incredibly relieved to find out he'd been taking his heart medicine all along, the fact was he'd run out soon. "I'll figure out a way to find more," she promised, taking his hand. His was so much larger than her own, and he'd always made her feel safe when he was near. Danny desperately wished that was still the case, except too much had happened, and what used to make everything okay simply wasn't enough anymore.

"My mom said you've spent some time with Caleb on the radio," Tom remarked to Bishop, as soon as they'd all sat down.

"Some," Bishop confirmed. "I haven't had as much time to learn the codes as I'd like. I don't have the opportunity to make it in to city hall very often, where the radio is." He leaned back in his chair and eyed Tom. "I've managed to help with some of the translations, though. What's your question?"

Tom wrung his hands together before clearing his throat, and Danny could tell he was nervous. She knew what he was going to ask and it was the type of thing where it might be better not to know. "When we were at the FEMA camp," Tom finally said. "They wouldn't allow us to use their radio at all. They insisted it was for military purposes only. So, we still don't know if Ethan's mom is alive or not. She was on her way to Hawaii when the ray hit."

Tane made a whistling noise and then shook his head before Bishop could answer. "I've helped Caleb, too, with some of the paperwork he's produced. One of the things I worked on was a list of stations he's contacted. I'm sorry," Tane added quietly. "Hawaii isn't one of them."

"That doesn't mean they're not there," Bishop offered. "In fact, based on what we've learned, I think Hawaii would be one of the safest places to be. We'll talk to Caleb tomorrow about it. I'm sure he'll have some ideas."

Tom was understandably disappointed by the news, and Danny wished there was something she could say. They all had so many questions, and they'd already gotten used to not having them answered instantly by googling or picking up a phone. She still had no idea how her co-workers and friends in Helena were doing, plus her mom and grandparents were also in Hawaii. Sam had already accepted that his wife was most likely dead, but he also had friends and colleagues in Helena. Sandy told them how unstable the city was, so going there wasn't really an option yet. At some point, they would, though it would probably be after winter. Until then, they'd have to figure out their roles in Mercy.

"Where *is* Ethan?" Sandy said, noticing the teen hadn't come outside with them.

"Bed," Tom said with a grin. "He's been going on about sleeping in his room since we left Vegas."

Studying her father in the glow of the fire, Danny was relieved to confirm that he still looked as good as he had when he first arrived at the house. She'd spent so much time imagining all the different ways he could be hurt or become sick that she was having a hard time believing he was okay. If Danny was honest with herself, she'd have to admit that he'd fared better than she had since the gamma ray.

Tane looked up and caught her staring. After a brief flash of concern clouded his dark features, he beamed a bright smile at her. Reaching out, he gently touched the knot on her forehead that was still noticeable. "You gonna tell me how you got that?"

Danny pulled away without meaning to, and then silently chastised herself. She'd been fiercely independent her whole life, even as a child, but the past few years she'd become more with-drawn and...shut down. While she was determined to tear down some of those walls, it was obviously going to take time as well as patience from the people around her.

"It happened at the FEMA camp," Tom offered. He was sitting on her other side and she turned to look at him gratefully. "While saving my butt," he added with a chuckle.

"Is that where you met?" Tane asked. They'd barely had time to catch up on the basics while eating, so Tane hadn't heard much yet.

"No," Danny said hesitantly. "It's a long story, Dad. I'll tell you more about it later. Basically, Sam and I came upon Ethan after he and Tom had a run-in with some criminals. Then, Tom found us, and we all decided it made sense to travel together since we were headed the same way."

"That's definitely the condensed version," Sandy said with a hint of laughter and a tinge of cynicism.

Danny cringed. They'd already told Sandy and Bishop most of what happened. She was going to leave out the details of her and Tom's first encounter, but to her dismay, Tom told her everything. Right down to him tackling her and putting her face into the ground before she pulled the gun and nearly shot him. Danny figured it was some displaced need to confess everything he'd done wrong to his mom, but she was afraid it would just make things awkward between her and Sandy. Based on the older woman's comment, Danny guessed she was right.

"Yeah," Tom agreed with his mom, and Danny held her breath. "Let's just say that despite my misguided efforts, Danny still managed to save Ethan and reunite us."

Danny let out her breath, thankful she wouldn't have to go into some long, drawn-out explanation with her dad. She was already emotionally exhausted and the beer was making her sleepy.

"It sounds like you were lucky to have Danny around," Bishop said.

Danny began to grin, but her expression froze as several images came to mind. Blinking to clear her head, she took another long swallow of beer. "It went both ways," she finally said.

"What do you know about those men we saw in the mountains?" Tom asked, clearly thinking back over some of the same encounters as Danny.

"Not much," Bishop answered. He stood and tossed another log on the fire, sending a cascade of glowing embers up into the darkness. "There have been some random attacks on a couple of the other communities we've connected with through the Pony Express. They've avoided Mercy so far, but probably only because we've closed down our roads and have armed guards."

"There's been rumors of them being everything from the militia to our own military," Sandy added.

"They're neither," Danny said hollowly. "We've come across both, and those pigs are nothing more than thieves and killers. They aren't fighting for anything, and all they care about are themselves."

"Desperados," Bishop said, as he stared at Danny and Tom through the fire, and she thought the way he said the word implied he'd dealt with such men before.

"Desperados?" Sam asked, speaking for the first time since going outside. Grace had chosen to sit at his feet, and he rubbed absently at her ears. Danny noticed he'd been unusually quiet the whole day. She suspected Sam was thinking more about his wife, now that they'd stopped running.

"It means a desperate or reckless criminal," Bishop explained.

"Seems fitting," Danny agreed. She watched as Sandy reached out to take Bishop's hand, apparently drawing comfort from the contact. It was clear the two had gotten close over the past two weeks.

"I don't care what we call them," Tom said solemnly. "So long as we do something about them."

"Like what?" Tane asked.

Tom glanced over at Danny, and then Bishop. "I know the trail they're using to move back and forth between the freeway and their camp."

"So?" Sandy said, her voice strained. "You said yourself there was upwards of a dozen armed men. What do you want to do, attack them?"

"The riders went missing somewhere along the freeway between Helena and Mercy, right?" Tom asked Bishop, ignoring his mom's question.

Bishop nodded. "We got confirmation from the station in Helena that the riders had made it there and were headed back." When Danny raised her eyebrows at him, he explained, "We were able to get the station set up with a ham radio."

Rubbing his hands together, Tom then held them out toward the fire to get warm. "That makes sense. The trail puts out about forty miles south of town. I'd be willing to bet that's where the riders were ambushed, and probably where they'll be waiting to jump the next riders, too."

Bishop downed the last of his beer, stood, and then went to get three more bottles from the nearby picnic table. Returning with them, he handed a fresh one to both Tom and Danny. "You're thinking we get there first?"

Danny watched as the two men exchanged a silent, knowing look. They were both men with strong personalities and opinions, and she was thankful they appeared to be on the same page.

Popping the top off the bottle, Tom tipped his head at Bishop. "I think it's time someone shut them down."

Her pulse quickened at the thought of going after the thugs she'd seen butcher the two riders from Mercy. Danny knew she should probably be troubled that it excited her. After all the talk of wanting nothing more than to reach Mercy and find some peace, in less than twenty-four hours, they were already planning yet another fight. Maybe that was simply the way of things now.

As Danny contemplated the emotions she felt, she realized that it wasn't the thought of killing someone that thrilled her. It was because they were finally on the offensive. Instead of running and fighting for their lives, they were getting a chance to stand their ground and take back some control by making the first move.

Leaning back in her chair, Danny raised her bottle to Tom. He held her gaze for a moment, and wisely didn't attempt to talk her out of getting involved. Instead, he tapped his drink against hers in a toast, his face shadowed in the flickering firelight.

"Here's to a successful hunt," she murmured, her voice low and dangerous.

CHAPTER 9

JAMES
>Master Sergeant, US Marines, 1st Force Reconnaissance
>Cheyenne Mountain Base, Colorado

THE ACCOMMODATIONS JAMES and his 1st Recon Unit were assigned sat on top of Cheyenne Mountain, which was how James wanted it. He couldn't handle the thought of sleeping underground, and had made it well known to Colonel Walsh when he'd told the team they would be staying there indefinitely.

The building couldn't be called a barracks, as it was much nicer than what the word normally referred to. It was a single-level structure with six bedrooms, a full kitchen, and a central living space. James was told it was previously used for visiting personnel, or dignitaries and their entourages who chose not to stay in the mountain. Apparently, he wasn't the only soldier who suffered from claustrophobia.

While the electrical system had been fried the same as any other building that wasn't shielded, free-standing lights had been brought in and were plugged into their own generator. Considering they had real beds, as well as space heaters for when it got chilly at night, they pretty much had all the comforts of home.

Except it wasn't home. James put a worn picture of his wife and daughter back into his wallet and walked out into the central room. He'd been doing a lot of thinking, and it was time to have a talk with his teammates and friends.

"Hey." Jay was already there, working on a sudoku puzzle. "What's up, Sarge?"

"Where's Lucas?"

Jay frowned at him. He didn't usually call them by their first names when in uniform of any sort, unless something was going down. "He's, uh, in the head."

Sergeant Lucas O'Grady walked out then, a hunting magazine in his hand. "Don't know what I was thinking," he mumbled, tossing the magazine onto a table. "Too dark to read anything in there without a flashlight."

"You hear about the attack on the FEMA shelter in Arizona this morning?" James asked, watching their faces closely.

Jay nodded. "Things are heating up."

Lucas sat across from Jay and he looked up at James, his lips pursed. "You know, for a secret facility, they're not very good at keeping secrets."

Jay threw his pen at him. "It's not a secret anymore, you moron."

"He's got a point," James said, interrupting their banter. "If you think about it, there's only one source of information both coming in and going out of this mountain. They got a report on the wire this morning and by dinner, everybody knows about it. Only reason that happens is because they *want* everyone to know about it."

Lucas was pointing at him and bobbing his head in agreement. "Exactly! I don't like it, man. It smells funky."

"Why?" Jay asked, leaning over to retrieve his pen. "What's the point?"

James crossed his arms over his broad chest and narrowed his eyes. "Because information is power. Let's take a walk."

Jay and Lucas exchanged a puzzled look, but didn't question their sergeant. Wordlessly, they followed him outside and across a small patch of grass that served as a green space, and then onto the tarmac. James didn't speak until they'd passed their Huey and stood on the edge of the hill, overlooking the valley.

"We're deep into something none of us wants to be involved in," he said stoically.

"You think our quarters are bugged or something?" Jay asked, glancing back nervously over his shoulder.

"Highly unlikely," James said, still staring out at the darkening landscape. "But I'm suddenly feeling a bit paranoid."

Lucas swallowed audibly and shoved his hands deep into the pockets of his fatigues. "Since when do *you* get paranoid, Sarge?"

"Since I found this." He turned then and silently held up a small piece of rolled-up paper. It was a narrow strip just wide enough to accommodate two rows of typewritten words.

Jay took it from him with a scowl and clumsily unrolled it between his fingers. "Next asset is a governor. Missions = lies. Time to choose sides. Admiral assassinated. All who oppose will die. Dad is alive." Jay's expression was pained as he stared at James. "Where'd you get this?"

James sighed and took it back, quickly stuffing it into his pocket. "When I got back from lunch, my Glock was out of the rack and set on my bed."

"Who'd touch your gun, man?" Lucas whispered, looking more concerned with each passing minute.

"No one," James said curtly. "That's the point. I figured I better break it down since I didn't know if someone had messed with it, and that's when I found it. In the barrel."

"That's some serious 007 shit right there," Jay said, rubbing his jaw and copying Lucas by looking behind them.

"I never was a fan of spy drama," James said dryly. "I prefer a more direct approach. You know, as in, say it to my face and let's be done with it. I'm not buying into this cloak-and-dagger bull."

"It doesn't even make much sense," Lucas said, mulling it over. "So what if the next asset is a governor? What admiral was killed, and which sides? And if that was meant for you, why are they talking about your dad?"

James huffed once and glanced at Jay. His friend had been smart enough not to push the issue about his dad being on the Survivor List, and agreed not to tell the rest of the team. Now things were going from weird to bizarre, fast, and James needed help figuring it out. "The last asset was my father," he said bluntly.

Lucas took a step back and needed all of about ten seconds to process the information before moving beyond it. "I knew your dad was in the military, man, but why would he be on this list?"

His friend's ability to take in the big picture rapidly was the main reason James was pulling him in. "I honestly don't know. He's been involved in some black-ops stuff, but I'm not aware of anything that would earn him a spot on the most-wanted list. I figure he either knows something that the government believes will be critical in our rebuilding, or else it's too dangerous for him to fall into the wrong hands."

"Namely, anyone other than our own military," Lucas added.

"At least you know he's alive," Jay offered.

James would have smiled in agreement if it weren't for the hard knot in his gut. It had started forming when he first unrolled the note and had been growing ever since. "Why would a governor be important?"

Lucas squinted at him, thinking about it. "Because they now represent what's left of the civilian government. Something the brass seems to be at odds with right now."

"I don't follow," Jay complained.

"After the president and vice president, the senate is next in line," James said, trying to follow his friends train of thought.

"Yeah," Lucas confirmed. "The senate was in session when the flashpoint happened, so we should consider them gone. That would make the governors next up."

"So?" Jay asked, clearly growing agitated. "Why do we care? We're under martial law; it doesn't matter how many governors are left."

"Actually, it does," Lucas countered. "Since I seem to be the only one who understands the government we're sworn to serve, I'll explain it to you." When James glared at him, Lucas threw his hands up defensively. "Okay! I'll keep it simple. Basically, the governors can all declare themselves senators and then, if enough of them get together, they can basically appoint one of them as the new president."

"Who could then overturn martial law and reinstate civilian authority," James finished, grasping the magnitude of the position they were in.

"So, you think our next asset is going to be one of these governors, and if our mission is a lie—"

"Then we aren't really going to be helping them," James interrupted Jay. "We're being used to shut it down."

"The admiral?" Jay asked.

"Still no clue."

"Again," Lucas said, throwing his hands up in the air. "Unlike you two, I'm actually friends with our pilot."

James shook his head. "And this matters because?"

"Our pilot?" Lucas interrupted, pointing over at the Huey. "Lieutenant Jeff Carpenter. You know, the guy who's been risking his butt on every mission we've been out on? Yeah, that one. Well, I talked to him today."

"And?" James pushed, losing his patience. It wasn't the time for twenty questions.

"He told me about how he flew one very pissed-off Admiral Baker to FEMA Shelter AZ1 two days ago."

"Baker," James muttered. "Isn't he one of the higher-ups here?

"He's one of the command chiefs," Jay confirmed. "They've got his picture hanging in the mess hall with the other three."

"Why would an admiral go to a FEMA shelter?" James asked, the knot growing a little bigger.

"According to him, and the earful he gave the whole crew during the flight, it was because he didn't get along with General Montgomery and his…command decisions," Lucas said, confirming what James already suspected.

"I'm guessing he was 'opposed'," Jay said with angst. "And that maybe he happened to be one of the casualties in the attack we were all sure to be made aware of."

James looked at each of his friends and teammates in turn, knowing they'd support him no matter what he decided. "I have a mission briefing with the general tomorrow."

"What are you going to do?" Lucas asked, going back to glancing over his shoulder.

A light breeze kicked up then, carrying with it the faint smell of the smoke that still lingered in the valley. It was a stark reminder that while they enjoyed the luxuries of power and comfort, everyone else around them still suffered. "First, we'll carry out our mission and get the governor, but we'll be making a detour before taking the asset anywhere."

Jay and Lucas both lifted their chins in response, and any sign of flippancy or fear dissipated from their demeanors. "Yes, sir," they said in unison.

James, encouraged by the show of support, gave a curt nod back. "For whatever reason, whoever gave me this warning feels my father is important in all of this, and I think I know where to find him."

CHAPTER 10

EDWARD
Oregon Coast

EDWARD LIT another candle and then pocketed the lighter as he shuffled slowly across the shadowy family room. The house groaned around him, making sounds he'd never heard come from it before. That was saying a lot, since he and his wife had lived there for over fifty years.

The age-old saying that it was always darkest before the dawn was proving to be true. The unbelievable storm had been raging all through the night, and now that they were finally, at long last, inching toward sunrise, Edward couldn't seem to keep the darkness at bay.

"Edward?" Margaret's voice was small and timid. It was yet something else Edward had never heard before, not even during the past eighteen days, after the end of the world. His wife was scared.

Stubbing his toe on a table as he fumbled in the dark, Edward bit back the blasphemous words threatening to tumble out and hopped the last few feet to the couch. His old bones creaked when he lowered himself next to Margaret, another reminder of his eighty-four years on the blasted planet.

"I'm here," Edward said, entwining his hand with Margaret's gnarled fingers. In addition to her failing sight, rheumatoid arthritis was busy sucking the life out of her joints. He'd refused to put the love of his life into assisted living, even when her memory started to fade and he would sometimes find her wandering the beach, unsure of where she was.

"It's only a storm," he said soothingly. Except that Edward wasn't so sure. Their home on the Oregon coast was solid and built to withstand the storms the Pacific Ocean sometimes hurled their way, but the tempest screaming at the doors was unlike anything he'd experienced. Not even in Alaska, or Florida, or all the foreign seas he'd sailed while in the Navy. It was…malevolent.

The storm surge was the first real sign that it was coming. A monstrous influx pushed ahead of the low pressure that had swelled around their five-acre property and cut off any escape, though attempting to leave was never a realistic consideration. On the other rare occasions that the winding country road was flooded by local streams after heavy rains, they couldn't even get through in a vehicle. This was much worse and didn't seem to be getting any better.

Since the event, Edward and Margaret hadn't been able to leave their home. The nearest town was a ten-minute drive and while Edward might have managed the walk if given enough time and favorable weather, he couldn't leave his wife alone for that long.

They were prepared. At least, Edward had always thought they were well prepared for any unforeseen disasters. Living on the West Coast for over half a century, the couple was well versed in all of the potential threats. They'd been through the eruption of Mount St. Helens, weathered the threat of a tsunami on more than one occasion, and had their fair share of power outages. In addition to sitting on top of the most dangerous subduction zone in the world, they also had several active volcanos close enough to warrant preparedness. They had a storm wall installed between their home and the wide, white-sand beach they were blessed to own. They had an expensive generator, lived on a well and septic, used solar panels, and had vast gardens that helped stock their root cellar.

Less than three weeks after the lights went out and they were cut off from any supplies, Edward knew that it wasn't going to be enough. Nothing they did could have prepared them for what happened, although he wasn't sure exactly what it was. Certainly, some neighbors had stopped by and they'd conversed about what was being said by people in town or those passing through. It was hard to filter out the tales from the reality, though the most likely scenarios presented were either some sort of radioactive wave from space, or a coordinated attack.

For Edward and Margaret, the what didn't really matter so much. They would run out of food and a means to get fresh water long before that would be of any significance. Another monstrous gust of wind shook the walls, threatening to rip them apart. Perhaps the food and water didn't matter, either.

The west coast of North America didn't usually get hurricanes, since the water wasn't warm enough to feed the storm. Every once in a great while, California could see the tail end of a typhoon sucked up from farther south, though that was nothing compared to what currently raged.

"Are the kids coming?" Margaret murmured, leaning into Edward. "I hope they aren't getting too wet. I'll need to turn the oven down so the turkey doesn't get dry."

Edward closed his eyes and tried to settle his thoughts. He'd rather deal with the storm than his wife's failing mind. "No, my dear. The children are safe."

There was a sudden lull in the howling, and then the atmosphere seemed to change as the air itself grew dense. In the shock of the silence, Edward looked down at Margaret's frail form enveloped in his arms and knew they were on a precipice. He thought back over all the special phases of their lives. The births of their children, the countless holiday dinners, camping trips into the mountains. The death of a grandchild, and the marriage of another. The first time he held his great-grandson. A faint smile was tugging at his lips when the pent-up breath of the night was released, and slammed into their home with a force only Mother Nature could produce.

"No!" he protested, angry that of all the many trials they had overcome, it would be the sea, their refuge, that would claim them in the end.

Margaret screamed as the windows imploded and the roof began to lift, and Edward squeezed his arms even tighter to spare her as much as possible. The storm was inside then; cold tendrils of the night that reached out and embraced him in a deadly caress, tearing at his clothes to expose his flesh. The candles were instantly snuffed out, plunging them into an eternal darkness.

They were but one house of thousands in the path of the hurricane's destruction, and it was only the first of many that would reshape the West Coast of America.

CHAPTER 11

GENERAL MONTGOMERY
Cheyenne Mountain Complex, Colorado

GENERAL MONTGOMERY LED the way through the secondary blast doors of Cheyenne Mountain, and then watched the expression on Corporal Dillinger's face as the internal mechanism groaned until the rods slid into place, effectively sealing them inside.

"Ahem." Corporal Dillinger tugged at his uniform and took a moment to gather himself before meeting the general's inquisitive stare. "A very...interesting sensation."

A rare smile softened the general's features. He appreciated the honest reaction. Most attempted to shrug off the discomfort of being shut inside the granite bunker. It was much better, he'd come to understand, to simply accept the low-level sense of doom and heaviness as a part of the experience. "You're at the mercy of the mountain now," he said dryly.

The general had personally met Dillinger on the tarmac. The

gesture was nothing more than a maneuver to briefly bolster the man's feeling of importance and loosen his tongue. Although, Montgomery was looking forward to giving him a tour of the complex. He enjoyed strolling the numerous, cavernous rooms and didn't have many opportunities to do it. "Have you had breakfast?" he asked, always the gracious host.

"Yes, sir," Dillinger barked. "Before leaving Peterson this morning. Though they clearly still have some obstacles to overcome, I'd say they've got the civilian unrest under control. In that part of Colorado Springs, anyway."

Montgomery scoffed in response. He didn't need, nor did he ask the corporal for a report on the state of his city. He could have had Dillinger brought straight to the mountain the night before, and given him much nicer accommodations. However, the general saw no reason to provide the corporal any unnecessary reasons to inflate his already healthy ego. He made a point, therefore, of establishing right away that the lowly FEMA shelter commander wasn't worthy of a port in the mountain. He could wallow below, and come only once beckoned. It made the current meeting more compelling. Dillinger was a grunt, and the general knew how to deal with them. It was all about posturing and respect.

After an hour, the general had led Corporal Dillinger through countless tunnels and rooms of various sizes. His personal favorite, the underground lake, had the expected effect, so by the time they left, Dillinger was noticeably silent.

As they ascended back the way they'd come, Montgomery waited, letting the minutes roll by until the other man finally cleared his throat. "Something on your mind, Corporal?"

"Well, sir, I can't help but think that you had me flown all the way down here for something other than a tour."

Again, with the bluntness. A corner of his mouth turned up; Montgomery glanced back over his shoulder. "One of the reasons I wanted to show you this facility is because my gut tells me you're a man who appreciates parallels."

"Sir?" Dillinger sounded genuinely perplexed.

"Take this bunker, for example." Stopping, General Montgomery turned to face the corporal, his expression stoic. "Right now, we are standing in the heart of a mountain. A literal marvel of mankind's ingenuity. It is likely the only place on Earth still functioning at such a capacity, and yet..." Twisting slightly, he lifted an arm and pointed at red words that had been painted on the wall years earlier.

Without power it's just a cave

"You're right, Corporal. I did summon you for a reason." Montgomery folded his arms over his chest. "I've been impressed with your continued progress at the shelter, as well as your ongoing requisitions. I read the latest reports yesterday morning regarding the cattle and farms in the neighboring towns of Monida, and I wanted to talk with you about heading up a task force to implement the same strategy on a broader scale."

Dillinger looked from Montgomery, to the red words on the rock, and then back at the general again. "Yes, sir. I'd be honored. And I understand."

"Do you?"

Dillinger shifted his feet slightly but didn't look down at them. Yes. He understood the game very well. "Without a show of increasing power now, we risk being reduced to nothing more than an army of aimless men, instead of an assemblage of warriors."

Montgomery gave one curt nod in confirmation, while resisting the urge to correct the other man. Let Dillinger and his men think of themselves as warriors, if that's what they needed. However, for the general and his crusade, it was more about becoming a sovereign regime.

"Tell me about the resistance you met," Montgomery asked as be began walking again. "The report was vague."

Dillinger waved a hand dismissively. "It was a couple of days ago. The owner of Duke Ranch is a pigheaded, obstinate man. Refused to hand over the requested cattle. It was unfortunate, really. No one had to die. It was over quickly and we're now using the farm as an additional center of operations for the area."

"Looked like a good spot for one on the map I have," the general said with approval.

"It isn't without its drawbacks," Dillinger mumbled.

"Such as?"

"Those farmers have a strong sense of loyalty," the corporal explained, as if that were a bad thing.

Montgomery knew that was the very reason why it was essential to establish military authority in that part of the country right away. Control of the livestock and farmland would be critical in the years to come. "They're refusing to work?"

Dillinger nodded. "Most of them walked away instead of conceding, and there's concern they might regroup and try to eventually take their property back."

"We'll have to make sure that isn't an option," Montgomery replied. "Let's not discuss forced work camps yet, however. Let's start by trying to reason with them. Offer compensation, in the form of shelter, food, and medication. A few weeks out there on their own, I imagine you'll be able to entice a fair amount back without any further violence."

"There might be another element to factor in," the corporal said, and Montgomery stopped and looked back at him. He could tell that whatever it was, it warranted his attention.

"Yes?"

"While we were searching the Duke residence, we found some maps," Dillinger said, pausing to look up at the rock ceiling high overhead when the venting system moaned to life. "They were out in the open and had some very specific markings which I believe involves a rather impressively organized supply train called the Pony Express."

"The Pony Express?" Montgomery chuckled, finding it humorous that Dillinger would think some vain attempt at running mail could pose a threat.

"Well, it's a vague reference," the corporal said gruffly, clearly disliking being laughed at. "We've heard of it on multiple occasions now, and it appears to connect no less than four or five different communities. A form of networking to share needed goods and information."

General Montgomery canted his head slightly at the mention of information. He narrowed his eyes. "And you think this supply train could somehow lend assistance to our vagrant farmers? Help them to organize?"

"Perhaps," Dillinger said, clearly relieved that the general recognized his train of thought so easily. "It's already being seen as a sign of civilian success and is encouraging to the small communities that are scattered throughout the state of Montana and into Idaho."

Idaho. Montgomery frowned. Not a state he wanted associated with civilian organization and accomplishments. "I take it there's more to this?"

The corporal's lip twitched and his nostrils flared. "Yes, sir. We believe this Pony Express is originating from a small mountain town called Mercy. It also happens to be home to one of the largest cattle farms in that part of the state."

"Mercy," Montgomery muttered to himself. "Early on," he said, recalling the name. "We had some form of communication established with them. If I remember correctly, it has a population of barely more than five hundred and is deep in the mountains, isolated by a valley."

"Yes, sir. But the resources would outweigh the disadvantage of being remote."

Montgomery stared hard at the corporal. "I know I've read some reports mentioning Mercy more recently."

Dillinger hung his head for a moment and scratched at his jaw. "It was included in my report, sir, about the rancher who gave us so much trouble at the shelter."

The general raised his eyebrows.

"He's Thomas Miller. The owner of the cattle ranch in Mercy. And, it's also been under a self-imposed quarantine for nearly two weeks," Dillinger continued. But I believe—"

"So, this is personal," Montgomery spat.

The corporal's head snapped up and his eyes narrowed. "No, sir. But it is about me having personal *knowledge* of the town, the kind of man Miller is, and that he runs a very successful ranch."

"How successful?" Montgomery asked.

"At least twice the size of Duke Ranch."

General Montgomery carefully considered the information as the ground under their feet vibrated slightly, another unsettling component of the ventilation system. "Conceivably large enough to warrant lying about a contagion to keep the military out."

Dillinger smiled. "Yes, sir. I suspect so."

His mind made up, Montgomery pivoted, his shoes squeaking against the granite, and began walking back up the tunnel. The corporal scrambled to catch up and walk alongside him. "Okay, Corporal. Get me proof that Mercy is the base of operations for this Pony Express, and that the quarantine is a charade, and I'll give you the orders you want."

"I'll start right away," Dillinger said excitedly. "I mean, after we're done planning the next phase, sir."

Montgomery stopped in front of the underground diner, aptly named the Granite Inn Dining Room. "We can hammer that out over lunch," he scoffed. "I imagine it'll be a simple matter of logistics and getting you the manpower you need. Walsh will see to that. You can head back tonight, if you like."

Instead of being insulted by the quick dismissal, the corporal stood even straighter and gave a brisk nod of his head. "Yes, sir. I'd like to get back as soon as possible. Can I ask, sir, if the other helo is available? While I was happy to learn Malmstrom got one of their old birds flying, I can't say I'm convinced it'll stay in the air."

"No," Montgomery said unapologetically. "It's needed for an important assignment." As the corporal tried not to look put out, he decided to further establish the need to impress him. "And Corporal, for your pet project, I only want you using boots on the ground. No extra resources are to be pulled for this."

"Understood, sir," Dillinger answered without hesitation. "I've already got everything I need near Helena. A warrior knows how to be resourceful."

Montgomery hated to admit it, but he did admire the man's tenacity. Perhaps there was something legitimate to the corporal's concern. It certainly would be nice to secure a thousand or more head of cattle.

"I'll get you your proof in three days," Dillinger promised, his demeanor unflinching. "And then, I'll get you Mercy."

CHAPTER 12

Tom

Sheriff's Office, Mercy, Montana

IT WAS A WEIRD SENSATION, riding down the Main Street of Mercy on horseback. Other than when he'd been talked into a parade or two as a boy, it wasn't something Tom thought he'd ever do.

At the southern end of town, he and Bishop made a stop at the sheriff's office while everyone else continued on to the spring. It was still really early in the morning, but his mom said the sheriff was pretty much living at the station, so they figured he'd be there.

Sure enough, Sheriff Waters emerged from the back room with a steaming cup of coffee in hand shortly after the front door chimed, announcing their arrival. "Tom. Bishop," he mumbled, lifting the cup in their direction. "Would you like some coffee? It's good. You know, being the coffee addict that I am, one of my earlier concerns after the power went out was that I wouldn't be able to brew a pot anymore. Why I've never used a French press,

I couldn't tell ya. Always took the instant packets when I went hunting. Anyway," he continued after taking another long sip from the mug, "best darn stuff I've ever had. Thank God Mr. Sullivan had a couple of crates of beans in his storeroom. Although, I figure we'll have to learn how to grow and make our own at some point."

"Sure, Sheriff. I'll take a cup," Tom said, enticed by the smell and entertained by the dialogue. Though the sheriff hadn't lived in Mercy for all that long, they had gotten to know each other reasonably well. The man had the unique ability to always be present in the moment. To slow things down and focus on what most others would pass over. Tom suspected it came from being a cop in a big city for so many years before he moved to Mercy.

Bishop held a hand up. "You know I don't usually drink it."

"Yeah, well, you're an odd man," the sheriff chuckled. "Come on back into my office, guys. I'm glad you stopped by. I wanted to talk with you, Tom."

Tom followed the older man into the large room with a bay window that overlooked Main Street. It allowed in enough light to reveal a cot in the far corner, and a scattering of personal belongings on the couch and counter. Tom helped himself to the coffee, and then chose to stand since there really wasn't anywhere to sit.

"Sorry about the mess," Sheriff Waters muttered as he leaned on the edge of his mahogany desk to face them. "I usually tidy up before anyone comes in."

"We're not here to judge your housekeeping abilities," Tom said with a grin.

"But we do need to talk about a few things," Bishop added in a more serious tone.

The sheriff sat his mug down and crossed his arms while nodding his head. "I figured you would. Tom, we're all glad you're back, of course, and I hope you understand why we're in need of your cattle. I'm sure your mom explained we've had her full cooperation?"

"She did," Tom confirmed. "Honestly, I'm on board with the whole exchange plan, Sheriff. I saw enough out there to be able to say with certainty that the only way we're going to survive and preserve our town is to do it together. Having said that, I want it understood that Miller Ranch won't be a part of any forced participation."

"Now Tom, the council—"

"The council knows nothing about your and the mayor's plan to move to stronger tactics should the need arise," Tom interrupted, his voice gruff. "I get where you're coming from, Sheriff...I do. You can try and hide behind the excuse that it's what's best for the town all you want; it still comes down to why we fight to live and also how we do it. It can't be at the cost of others' lives or freedom. Not when we have other options."

"Well, I'm glad to see you have all our problems figured out in the twenty-four hours you've been back." The sheriff rose slowly and stretched his back, wincing. "That cot is doing a real number on me."

Bishop and Tom exchanged a look, but remained silent as the lawman for Mercy mulled over his response while slowly going through the motions of preparing more coffee for the press. Dumping the old grounds in the garbage, he took the kettle off a tiny butane camping stove where it was heating.

It wasn't until he'd poured the water and moved the pot aside that he finally addressed them. "Okay. I can live with that, and I suppose it was wrong of Patty and I to discuss such things outside of the council. You know me, Tom. A politician I'm not. I'm happy to leave the policy-making to others while I focus on upholding 'em."

While Tom never thought the sheriff would offer much resistance, he was still relieved. They all needed to be on the same page to make things work.

"And Patty?" Bishop asked.

"Patty's tired," Sheriff Waters said bluntly. "Don't judge her too harshly. You haven't been here. She's held up better than most would, with more weight on her shoulders than anyone should ever have to bear. She won't disagree with you, Tom," he continued, resigned. "You offer the council a way to keep us all fed this next year and Patty will be happy to go along with whatever your plan is. That's all she wants."

"We need to talk with you about those men we encountered in the mountains," Bishop said, changing the subject. Tom was coming to understand that Bishop was exceptionally organized in his thinking and execution. Since they'd gotten the response they needed from the sheriff regarding the cattle, it was time to move on to their next objective. The speed with which he shifted tactics and direction wasn't a personality trait Tom expected from a man who worked a cushy desk job in the city.

"What about them?" Sheriff Waters asked, pushing the plunger down on his brew.

"Something needs to be done about them," Tom said brusquely. "Soon."

The sheriff peered at Tom over his steaming mug and raised his eyebrows. "And what sort of something would that be?"

"Our understanding is that the next rider is still scheduled to go out in two days," Bishop said.

"Yup," the sheriff confirmed. "I talked it over with Barry, the guy riding next, and he's still willing to run it so long as we send a few extra guns out with him. One of my deputies and two others already volunteered. We've been waiting on some much-needed meds and can't put this run off."

"Good," Tom said. "Then we'll only have to scrounge up a few more."

"A few more what?" Sheriff Waters pushed, his patience with them clearly running out.

Bishop took a step forward. "A few more volunteers. We figure there's a good chance the desperados know the route and maybe the schedule. They're using the trail that connects that valley to the freeway. Odds are they'll be waiting either just north or south of it."

"Only, we'll be prepared," Tom cut in. "And this time, they'll be the ones ambushed."

Sheriff Waters set his coffee down and tugged at his gun belt before hooking his thumbs in it, squinting at Tom. "Aren't you the one who just got done lecturing me about how we can't do anything that jeopardizes the freedom or lives of anyone? And not a minute later you're suggesting we ambush and kill upwards of a dozen men?"

"I'd say closer to nine or ten," Tom corrected. "And this would qualify as one of those situations that can't be avoided."

"They attacked us first," Bishop said, staring back unflinchingly at the sheriff. "I talked with Jed and he confirmed that he was jumped near where that trail comes out. He was lucky the priest came along when he did, and that there weren't more of them. They've already killed two of our riders, and they'll kill more if we let them. Eventually, they might get bold enough to come to Mercy. If we act now, we still have the advantage and the element of surprise. With more time, their numbers will likely grow and there's a good chance they'll also get more organized."

"Oh, I see," the sheriff huffed. Moving behind his desk, he stood staring out at Main Street. "Sounds like you've got all the justification you need."

"Sheriff." Tom walked around the other end of the desk so they were facing each other. "We need your support in this."

Sighing, the sheriff ran a hand along the edge of his unshaven jaw, clearly unhappy with the position he found himself in. "I'm not saying I disagree," he finally said, still staring outside. "Hell, I'll even offer to go myself. One of those men they killed was a friend of mine, Tom."

The sheriff turned to look at him then, and Tom was reminded of some of the lighter conversations they'd shared over the past few years, back when things were normal. Waters was a good, fair man, and it was unsettling to see the scorn in his eyes.

"I just want to make sure you're doing it for the right reasons."

"Our options are limited, as well as our reasons," Bishop answered for Tom. "Unless you want to drop the gag order and reach out to the military for help."

"Like I said," Sheriff Waters voice had grown more of an edge to it. "I don't disagree, and the military isn't likely to be a better choice."

"I think we can all agree on that," Tom said.

"What about the civilian government?" Bishop suggested.

Tom looked at him, surprised. It wasn't something Bishop had ever mentioned before and he felt like he was being blindsided. "What do you mean? Last I heard, the civilian government didn't exist."

"Maybe not at the federal level, but what about the states?" Bishop stood with his arms resting behind his back as he faced the other two men. "I'd imagine there's got to be some disagreement going on given how the military is literally invading their states. We've been going through all of this blind so far. I'm simply suggesting that we attempt to get a little broader focus."

Tom studied Bishop's face for a moment, trying to figure the older man out. All of a sudden, he was an advocate for the state government? His eyes narrowing, Tom carefully chose his words. "I don't see how we could possibly defend isolating ourselves from the military while at the same time trying to reach out to anyone else."

A light knock at the partially open door interrupted them,

and Tom turned to see a middle-aged man he'd never met before standing awkwardly in the doorway. "Uh, sorry to interrupt, Sheriff. I was on my way back to the church and thought I'd stop in to see if you're done writing your eulogy for Father White." His voice was a little too syrupy for Tom's liking and he would have never taken the man for a priest. Maybe an insurance salesman.

Sheriff Waters grunted and then sorted through some loose papers scattered on his desk. He didn't look too happy about it as he grabbed a page and then walked it over to the man. "Tom, this is Father Rogers, our new pastor," Sheriff Waters said as an afterthought while handing the priest the paper.

Father Rogers nodded in Tom's direction and folded the eulogy in half. "Nice to meet you," he said somewhat dismissively, before turning back to the sheriff. "Thank you, Sheriff. I'll be sure to have Madeline add this to the service."

As Tom watched the man leave, he noticed he was wearing regular street clothes and didn't have a collar or anything else to designate himself as a pastor. The bell chimed as he opened the front door, and Tom frowned. It hadn't rung when Father Rogers came in, making him wonder just how long the pastor had been standing there, listening to them.

CHAPTER 13

CHLOE
Natural Spring, Mercy, Montana

CHLOE LED Ethan to where all of the tools were stored, while glancing over her shoulder at the tumultuous sky. She was already getting stressed out over another storm that was forming, even though it was well south of the valley. "Here," she said, handing him a hammer. Ethan ignored the tool and moved past her to start rummaging through the large wooden box.

"I prefer this kind," he said, stepping back with something that looked more like a sledgehammer to Chloe. "And I'm guessing I'll probably need one of these, too." He held up a saw and grinned when she rolled her eyes. "What? You think I don't know my way around a toolbox, Chloe? You know who my dad is."

Snorting, Chloe snagged a bag of nails from Caleb before he went back to unloading more supplies from the nearby wagon.

The Spring Clearing, as they'd come to call it, was bustling with activity that morning. After the last storm, everyone decided that they should build a protective shelter over the main body of the spring.

Sam confirmed the night before that their suspicions were right about the rain. It was becoming toxic to the plants and fish, and could eventually contaminate their drinking water. Thankfully, the source of the water was deep inside the earth so they should be able to keep it drinkable by keeping most of the rain out. Sam suggested constructing the building a minimum of ten feet to either side, to avoid groundwater leaching in.

Chloe noticed where the stakes were set for the foundation poles, and figured it was going to be closer to fourteen feet, which would give them a sizeable building when they were done. Bishop mentioned using it to store some of the water, so they'd have a healthy supply in two different areas. Apparently, keeping all the goods in one place made it "vulnerable". To what, she wasn't sure and didn't ask. Some things were better left unsaid, and Chloe was trying really hard the past few days to be more optimistic.

Ethan picked up three eight-foot lengths of two-by-fours and they walked together over to where the construction was just getting underway. "I don't *think* I know anything about you," Chloe countered. "Except what your grandma told me, and what I could get from a year-old picture."

"Oh, yeah? And what was that?" Ethan asked, seeming amused by the conversation.

Chloe bit at her lip. She wasn't sure why, but there was something about the guy that threw her off. Her normal snark was markedly slow on the uptake and she was way overthinking what she was going to say. Maybe it was his broad shoulders, or incredibly enticing green eyes—

"Earth to Chloe," Ethan called, nudging her arm.

Blushing, she tried to recover any potential cool points that might remain. "Honestly? A kid about three inches shorter with a fondness for chess and an obvious wheeze."

"Ha!" Ethan chortled. "Yeah, Grandma likes to brag about how brilliant I am. I mean, she's right, but I'm more of an outdoors kinda guy than your normal nerd. I don't even play chess...much."

"Bring those over here!" Sam called to them as Grace ran up and tried to take one of the boards in her mouth.

"No, Grace!" Ethan ordered, laughing at the dog's antics. "Leave it. This isn't yours." Looking heartbroken, the retriever barked once and then ran off to find a real stick.

"She's a smart dog," Chloe giggled, and then slapped a hand over her mouth. She didn't giggle. *Ever.*

"Shh, don't let her hear you call her a dog." Ethan dropped the boards at Sam's feet and then gave the older man a mock salute. "We're here to do your bidding, sir."

Sam returned the salute with a small gesture toward his forehead and then pointed at the obnoxiously long hammer. Raising his dark eyebrows, Sam shook his head without comment.

Chloe had been around the four newcomers for barely more than twenty-four hours and she was already envious of their friendship. She'd only heard some of the things they'd been through together while on the road, and she suspected the rest was the sort of stuff that could make strangers closer than some families.

"Sandy said you have quite a bit of knowledge about the rain," Patty said in greeting as she approached the three of them. Chloe was happy the mayor was there that morning. She hadn't seen her much the past few days, and had been wanting to set up another time to go out to their place again to help in the garden. Sandy and Patty were a lot alike, but Patty had a way of engaging

Chloe in some fascinating conversations that reminded her of time spent with her dad. The last time she went over, they sat in Patty's garden pulling weeds for nearly two hours, talking the whole time about space, the universe, and what a black hole was.

"I don't know if I'd go so far as to call it knowledge," Sam replied, leaning on a shovel. "More of a supposition. There's probably more reliable information in the books at your school in town."

"Perhaps," Patty said while pulling on some work gloves. "Except that I can't have a conversation with a book, can I?" When Sam shook his head and smiled, she took a step closer and smiled at him. "I'd like to invite you to our next council meeting, tomorrow morning. Tom is already going and I think it would be very beneficial to get your input on some things, too."

Sam scratched his head and wrinkled his nose at her. "I'm not much for committees, Mayor. I've sat on enough to last a lifetime. What sort of input are we talking about?"

"Oh, nothing scary," she promised, waving a hand in the air. "A firsthand account from someone who understands a bit of the science behind what's happening would be very educational. Most of what we've garnered has been via some tapping on a ham radio and word-of-mouth from our Pony Express riders. We've been blessedly sheltered from a lot of what's going on, but I'm afraid it's also limiting our view, if you know what I mean."

"The view's just fine here in Mercy," Ethan offered. "Trust me."

"Well, I did hear someone asking about indoor farming," Sam said. "It might be something worth talking about, because if you're going to attempt it, you'll need to start soon before the ground pH is altered by the rain."

"See? That's exactly why we need your input!" Patty said, clapping her hands together enthusiastically. "We've already got some great greenhouses on a few farms, but I know we're going to have to do something on a much grander scale if we plan on feeding our whole community."

Chloe grinned as she watched Sam nod. The man was already sucked in over his head and didn't even know it yet. It was a talent of Patty's that Chloe suspected had helped make her successful as mayor.

"Maybe a few old barns?" Sam was obviously thinking out loud. "You're going to want to be close to a fresh water supply, of course, and have either sunlight or some sort of rigged artificial light, which would obviously be difficult. Solar panels?"

"How about a cave?"

Patty and Sam turned to look at Ethan, who shrugged at them. He pointed toward the mine opening. "Henry's Hollow. You know the story, Patty. The old miner, Henry, found it early on when they started that mine. It's bigger than two of the school gyms put together, and has a couple of natural chimney holes that let in some light."

"You've been in it?" Patty asked, her eyes wide.

"Of course!" Ethan said, as if offended, which made Chloe laugh. He narrowed his eyes at her before turning back to the mayor. "A lot of us kids have been at some point. It's our county version of a haunted house."

Chloe guessed he was referring to a sort of rite of passage. Like the more typical haunted house in the town where she grew up, where you're dared to go and touch it. Some kids took it further and threw rocks through the windows of the old, abandoned mansion, but Chloe refused to go along. Always the rebel.

"It's dangerous in there," Sandy said, joining their group. "When the mine was abandoned, they left a bunch of crap behind in that cave, including their old dynamite."

"So we clean it out," Sam suggested.

"You know how to handle old, crystallized dynamite?" Sandy asked.

When Sam shrugged his shoulders, Patty wasn't discouraged. "I'll bet our friend Bishop, as a civil engineer, knows a thing or two about handling explosives."

"I saw him and Tom ride up a few minutes ago," Sam said. Chloe noticed how he seemed to have forgotten everything he'd just said about not wanting to be on a committee, and was just as eager as Patty to take on the new project. "Let's go find Bishop and see what he thinks."

"Don't worry about us," Ethan called after the adults as they all walked away together. "We'll just stay here and build stuff, even though the cave was totally my idea."

Chloe chuckled, relieved it didn't come out as another giggle, and picked up the shovel Sam dropped. Normally, she didn't get along very well with guys who were younger than she, but Ethan was mature for his age. Maybe it was because of what happened to him in the past three weeks. "When's your birthday?" she asked without really thinking about it first.

Ethan looked at her in surprise, confused by the sudden change in subject. "Um, about ten days...I think. I'm still not real clear on what day it is."

"It's June 30th," Chloe explained. "And my birthday is next month."

"You'll be seventeen?" Ethan asked, sounding suddenly shy.

Chloe wagged her eyebrows at him and enjoyed seeing him squirm a little. "Nope. I will be an adult, so I believe that means you'll have to do what I say." He seemed to relax when she joked about their nearly two-year age difference. She was a little surprised to realize that it mattered to her that Ethan knew she didn't care he was younger. Because...she liked him. Against every rational thought she could have come up with over the past two weeks when imagining the boy and his dad traveling to get home against all odds, she liked Ethan.

"Tell ya what," Ethan said, putting an arm around her shoulders as they walked to where everyone was gathering to get further instructions. "If you promise to ignore our age difference, I'll give you a private tour of Henry's Hollow."

Enjoying the sense of security and belonging his closeness gave her, Chloe smiled up at him. "It's a deal."

CHAPTER 14

DANNY
Outskirts of Mercy, Montana

THE WAGON RATTLED over the gravel road, jarring Danny's bones with every little bump. She couldn't imagine how the pioneers rode for weeks on these things when there weren't even any roads. It made sense now, the pictures she'd seen of the weary travelers walking alongside the covered wagon, instead of inside.

A large container of water was carefully centered in the back of the cart, and secured with several straps to prevent it from shifting. It was the third run of the day to bring the much-needed spring water to the distribution center set up at the northern edge of town.

"You guys consider adding some sort of shock absorbers to this thing?" Danny said to her father, who sat next to her holding the reins. She was impressed with how comfortable and happy he still looked so late in the day. It was the first run she'd made with him and her backside was already sore.

Chuckling, he moved slightly on the creaky bench seat so he could face her while they talked. "I imagine this takes some getting used to. This new one is quite a bit smoother than the original."

Danny raised her eyebrows. "Really? I can understand why it broke apart, then." She regretted the words as she watched her father's face cloud. "Sorry, that didn't come out right. I know you lost some friends in the accident."

"We've all lost friends," Tane replied, facing forward again. "And loved ones." He glanced sideways then, and Danny knew he wanted to say something more but was holding back.

She wasn't taking the bait to start a deep conversation. That wasn't why she'd volunteered to ride with him into town. All Danny wanted was a few minutes of near-normalcy with her father. Although another storm was getting closer, the weather was holding for the moment. The sun was warm on their backs, the birds were singing, and little white fiber clouds from the cottonwood trees floated in the air around them. It was all set against the vivid backdrop that was the valley of Mercy. Every direction Danny turned, there were more majestic mountain ranges, the bases blanketed in evergreens. They rose to startling heights, bare rocks jutting up to form various craggy outcroppings that looked like they touched the sky. Except for the browning of certain types of trees, the wilderness appeared immune to the death and destruction that was raging in the rest of the world.

"It's easy to forget here," Tane said, accurately reading his daughter's silence.

Danny only nodded. She was afraid to speak, because then it would all be real again.

"You still haven't said anything about your mom or grandparents."

There it was. Danny took a collective breath. "I'm sorry."

Tane audibly sighed and it made Danny cringe. Her father had a way of saying more without any words. "I'm not fishing for an apology, Danny. I'm trying to figure out what's going on inside your head. I need to know you're okay."

"I'm sitting right here." She looked out at the passing scenery, anywhere except her father's face.

"That's not what I mean."

Danny clenched her jaw, and the bump on her forehead ached like a beacon that was still active in a storm. "I don't know what you want me to say. Are you upset that I'm leaving to go on the ambush?"

"You mean the raid?" Tane asked, his displeasure obvious.

"You don't want me to go," she accused, still watching the passing trees.

"I don't understand why you would want to go, but I'm not going to ask you to stay. You'd only resent me."

He was right, just not about the resentment. She closed her eyes, shutting out the sun and forcing herself to look inward. Danny had spent the past three weeks fighting to get to Mercy under the pretense of reaching her father because he needed her. Now that she was there and discovered how well he was doing, maybe she was continuing her search for…what, a purpose?

"Not everything has to be a fight." Reaching out, Tane took her hand and Danny felt like a child again, when the simple touch of her father made her fears fade away because she knew she wasn't alone.

The emotion was so powerful that it created a stabbing pain in her chest and stole her breath for a moment. He was right here. Her dad. Her family…her reason.

"I'm so sorry, *Makua Kane,*" Danny whispered, using the Hawaiian name for father, something reserved for times of endearment. Leaning against her dad's broad shoulder, she squeezed his hand in acknowledgement. "I *have* thought of mom, and grandma and grandpa. I believe in my heart that they're okay."

Tane squeezed her hand back. "Your heart has always had some pretty accurate radar. What is it telling you now, *keiki?*"

Danny grinned. It used to infuriate her when her father called her *keiki,* or child. "It's telling me that I need to remember what brought me here in the first place. Not to seek revenge for what happened along the way." When her dad glanced at her hopefully, she dropped his hand and gave him a quick hug. "You don't need to ask me to stay. My place is here, with you. I'm sure Tom and Bishop will have all the help they need."

Tane's smile was big and contagious. "You know, once we are caught up with the water today and have the second wagon and shelter at the spring built, we won't need the extra help."

"Already trying to get rid of me?" Danny joked.

The road leveled out as they reached the bottom of the hill, and Danny could see the school building and beyond it, what used to be a gas station. There were several people milling around it and the large parking lot across from it, where lines were forming for water. She was surprised at how many people there were. Even for a town with a population of around six hundred, it was clearly a monumental task to keep them all fed and provide them with fresh, drinkable water. Danny couldn't imagine what it must be like in the larger cities after so much time.

Tane gestured to the school. "Dr. Olsen could really use some help at the clinic. She's a great physician and there's one other nurse aside from Mayor Patty, but no one who has the sort of training in emergency medicine like you do."

"What about the fire department?" Danny asked, not sure what she thought of the idea. "I know they've got to be small, but don't they have any EMTs?"

"Whoa," Tane called out to the horses as they approached

their destination in the parking lot. "I imagine Chief Martinez must be certified, but I'm not sure about any of the others. They've only got a few responders and have really struggled to figure out a workable system."

Danny mulled it over as she jumped down and stretched out her legs. She watched while several organizers approached the wagon and immediately began to fill smaller containers full of water. Within minutes, they formed a type of water brigade and it didn't take long before the tank in the middle of the lot was filled enough for the line to start moving as people got their shares.

They did it without a lot of talking, and the water was handled like the precious commodity it was, so no more than a few drops were spilled. Danny was impressed with the camaraderie. There wasn't any pushing or shoving, or arguing over who got there first or that they wanted more. Although, she noticed there was a uniformed police officer standing by and watching. Danny imagined that things might have been a bit rougher in the beginning, and there was bound to be someone who wasn't as cooperative every once in a while, but to see what they'd accomplished was inspiring.

Strolling to the far side of the lot, Danny looked up Main Street and to where the fire station was located. She'd driven past the building numerous times over the past couple of years, but had never been inside. Thinking about getting back to the basics of being a responder had a certain appeal to it. Standing there, seeing the actual people of Mercy working together for something better sparked a flame that had long ago burned down to nothing more than a smoldering ember.

Danny wanted to help them.

$\mathcal{E}$THAN
Miller Ranch, Mercy, Montana

THE STORM BROKE LOOSE without much warning, and wind-driven rain lashed out at Ethan's face and tugged at his hat. The sky danced with the same odd-colored lightning as before, giving him flashbacks from when the tree fell on him. It was hard to believe that had only been four days ago.

Ethan struggled to control his horse and he had to admit he was thankful his dad insisted he not ride Tango. Tango wasn't trained for working around cattle, although Ethan had argued the best way to teach him was to just do it. It wasn't taking much to establish his arm still hurt, even when riding a well-trained cattle horse. Tango would have already dumped him. Several times.

"Ethan!"

He looked to where his dad was calling him, and saw that several cows had broken off from the main herd and were pressing up against a section of weak fencing. The rain was coming down so hard that it was difficult to see, even though it wouldn't be dark for a couple more hours.

Ethan urged his horse forward and together, he and his dad managed to corral the frightened cattle back in with the rest of the cows in the upper field. They weren't far from the lake and a decent distance from the barn. It was going to be a long, cold ride back once they were done.

When the storm had picked up speed and drawn closer late that afternoon, his dad pulled him from his work at the spring. The ranch still had to be their first priority and they couldn't risk losing any of the cows. Especially not with them calving. Bishop and the others stayed to try and finish the covering before the rain hit, their group dinner cancelled.

"Let's ride the line!" Tom called, already turning back to the fence.

Line rider would be Ethan's primary job, now that he was back at the ranch. It was a tedious, lonely job of riding for miles, every day, checking the barbed wire fencing that marked the edges of most of their property. It would entail patrolling the boundary, turning back any stray cattle, and making what would likely be countless repairs. He would also always be checking on the condition of the grazing fields and water supply.

With such a huge spread, Miller Ranch usually employed two fulltime hands, one of whom did nothing but ride the lines. Ethan had helped the summer before and actually enjoyed it, except when there was bad weather. At the moment, his dad was only referring to the upper field, which was where most of the calving cattle were at since the lake provided them with a constant supply of water. Normally, they'd be down closer to the barn.

Thinking of the hired hands reminded Ethan of his conversation with Sam earlier that day. "Sam said he's going to stay in the bunkhouse!" he shouted to his dad, curious what he'd think about it. The bunkhouse was basically a room added on to the back of the barn. It was drafty and sparse, but had two beds and a good woodstove.

"I know," Tom answered, as they moved nimbly along the back of the field. "I guess he and Bishop have decided to become roommates."

"You gonna try and talk them out of it?" Ethan asked. While he hated to think of Sam basically living in a barn, it would be really nice to have his room to himself.

"No point in trying." Tom had to shout to be heard over the wind. "Bishop insists on giving me my room back, and I'm pretty sure Sam has already started to refinish the floors. They'll probably have it shaped up in no time, and then you'll want to move out there, too!"

A bolt of bluish lightning pulsed directly over them, branching out across the ravaged sky to strike at the side of the mountain, no more than a few miles away. Ethan ducked instinctively as the thunder crashed almost simultaneously. His horse lurched sideways, and he watched as his dad's reared up, screaming and eyes rolling.

"Whoa, Lilly!" Tom shouted, nearly coming unseated. The sure-footed horse sidestepped and then slipped in the pooling water before finally stamping her hooves and snorting loudly, while Tom expertly handled her, talking soothingly all the while.

Ethan was always enthralled when watching his dad on a horse. It was like the animal was an extension of him, instead of something he rode. Ethan was a good rider, but he knew he'd never match his dad's skill.

A gust of wind slammed into him, and Ethan turned his face into it, noticing the change in temperature. It was markedly warmer and coming from the opposite direction. His dad picked up on it, too.

"It's shifting," Tom said, his voice carrying more easily in the sudden lull as the wind died just as rapidly as it came.

Ethan watched in stunned amazement as the boiling clouds overhead began to *lift* above the undercurrent to form mammatus clouds, as Sam had called them. Fat, drooping bubbles like the underside of a frozen pond. The whole system moved to the east and took the rain with it, which could be seen as a wall of water working its way up and over the distant ridge.

In the storm's abrupt wake, the setting sun from the opposite direction burst through and cast long arms of light to chase after it. With the lightning still dancing among the retreating clouds, the contrasting images were like an apparition from another world.

"So, this is what it's going to be like from now on?" Tom said from below him. Ethan looked down to find his dad had dismounted and was staring up at the sky while talking, unable to look away.

Ethan dropped to the ground next to him without answering. There really wasn't anything to say. They were powerless to control any of it and had no option other than to accept it for what it was.

Tom shook his head and then removed his cowboy hat to push the hair out of his face. Ethan was surprised he hadn't cut it yet, and he'd never seen it so overgrown. With the beard and left-over bruising, his dad had never looked more the part of a rugged cowboy. "We'll just check the rest of this back fencing and call it good. Looks like there's clear skies now. For a little while, at least."

"I'll ride the north line tomorrow," Ethan offered, as they began to walk their horses. With over five thousand acres, it came out to roughly eight square miles of land. He could easily spend most of his time on the one task.

"Sounds good," Tom agreed. "Except we're going to need to get the rest of the hay cut as soon as possible."

Ethan groaned. Cutting and baling hay was hard enough when you had working farm equipment. The idea of going at the field with a sickle and ball of twine made his hands ache. "How much did Grandma get done? And is it possible to get that old tractor running? I mean, how many electrical parts can be in it? It's ancient."

Tom chuckled and replaced his hat. "Mom only got the first quarter of the crop done. She was two days into it when the gamma ray hit. And as to the tractor, I guess Bishop has spent several hours going over it with the same thought. He's got some parts on our most-wanted list for the Pony Express riders, but it's not very likely we'll ever get them. Unfortunately, being so old makes it harder, because even when the power was on, finding spare parts for it was a trick."

Ethan kicked at a rock and watched it roll through the grass that was heavy with rain. The ten acres of hay was what they used to feed the cattle over the winter, and to supplement the grass year-round. With the acid rain effects already starting to show, there was no telling what would happen to the crop in the years to come, or if there would even continue to *be* a crop. It reminded him of the conversation earlier that day with Sam.

"You hear about the whole indoor farming thing?"

Tom tugged at a loose stretch of wire and then went back to Lilly for his tools to tighten it up. "Sam mentioned it when I saw him this afternoon. He's going to talk about it more tomorrow at the council meeting, but I don't see how we could possibly grow enough hay inside anywhere."

"Henry's Hollow," Ethan offered. "It's got to be close to three acres, don't you think?"

"I've got a farm out here to worry about," Tom said, twisting the wires tight while deftly handling the tools. "We need to focus on saving the hay that's already here, and that means getting an early start on cutting tomorrow. Don't worry about the line for now. Bishop and I will help with the hay tomorrow, so we should get a good jump on it before we leave."

Ethan looked back when his dad stopped talking and saw that he was staring at him, waiting for a response. "Okay…I'm sure Chloe will help me."

"Ethan, we haven't really talked about what's happening with the ambush."

Ethan studied his dad's face for a moment, gauging his reply. "What's there to talk about?"

Tom shoved the tools back in the leather saddlebags and then frowned at him. "I know you're probably expecting to go, but I need you to stay here."

"Still trying to protect me," Ethan muttered before walking away. He didn't even want to go, but the fact that his father continued to treat him like a child was frustrating.

"Of course, I am," Tom said, his voice rising. Falling in step alongside him, he reached out to stop Ethan. "I'm your dad and I'm always going to protect you. That's my job. But that's not what this is about. I know you can take care of yourself, Ethan, you've proven that. More than once. You might even have a valid argument that you've done a better job than me these past few weeks."

Ethan grunted at that and even grinned a little. "Honestly, Dad, I wasn't planning on going."

Tom looked at him in surprise. "I figured I'd end up having to chain you to a fence somewhere."

Ethan's smile faded. "I've seen enough death. I know we need to stop these guys, and I'm probably being a coward. But, as much as I wanted Decker to die, and even dreamed about different ways to do it, when I saw him dead, I didn't feel any better. I just felt empty and I don't want to feel that way anymore."

"That's not being a coward," Tom said, in a way he'd never spoken to Ethan before. It was how he talked to Sam, or Danny, or the other people he respected. "I need you here to take care of your grandma, and to watch over the farm. She's lost too much and I can't intentionally put you in harm's way. We can't do that to her."

As Ethan nodded, Tom reached out and pulled his hat off, ruffling Ethan's hair the way he used to do when he was little. It was such a simple gesture, and one that spoke of a time back when they were always together and before the world had gone crazy. Ethan stepped forward and welcomed the strong embrace of his dad as he took one long, shuddering breath. He finally understood that being a man wasn't necessarily about being a rock. Sometimes, like his dad, he was beaten down or even wrong, but his dad was still there. He was always there.

Reluctantly, Ethan moved out of his dad's arms. He was ready to step up and be there for both his dad and grandma, and the people of Mercy who were counting on their farm to help keep them alive.

"It's going to be okay," Tom said, his voice raspy.

Ethan drew from his dad's strength and the knowledge that he always followed through on his promises.

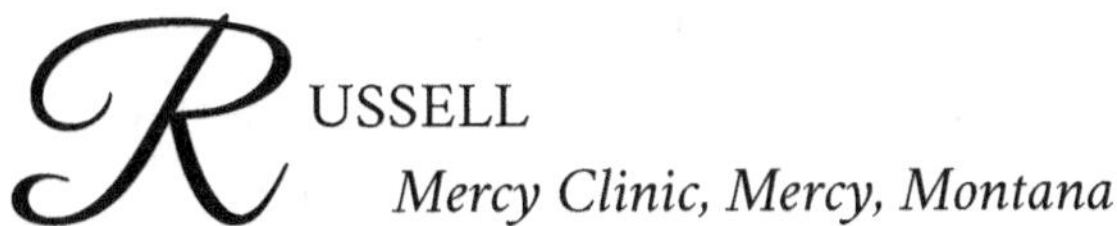

CHAPTER 16

USSELL
Mercy Clinic, Mercy, Montana

DANNY LATU WAS like no other creature Russell had encountered before. Her deep voice first caught his attention when he entered the clinic and heard her talking with Melissa. But it was her dark, exotic features that captivated him. As he drew close, he saw that he was only a couple of inches taller than her and her shoulders were nearly as broad as his. Yet, she somehow managed to look feminine.

"Father Rogers," Dr. Olsen beamed when she saw him. "It's good to see you. I wasn't sure if you'd be by this morning."

"Melissa, I've told you a dozen times to call me Russell," he said humbly, knowing she'd be happy he used her first name. "And I'm a little hurt you thought I'd abandon you so easily. I know how busy you are and I'd never miss an excuse to spend some extra time here."

Melissa blushed and then seemed to realize she'd failed to introduce him to the new, mysterious woman. "Oh! Fath—I mean, Russell, this is Danny Latu. She just got here a couple of days ago. Her dad is Tane Latu. Can you believe she traveled all the way from Salt Lake City, after her plane died at the airport? That's probably even farther than you made it."

"Salt Lake," Russell said, fully turning his gaze on her for the first time. Reaching out to shake her hand, he noted what a firm grip Danny had. "Why, we weren't all that far from each other at some point."

Danny cocked her head questioningly at him. "Oh?"

"Yes, I came north from the southwestern corner of Wyoming," Russell explained. "Most of it was spent on a bike."

"We used Interstate 15," Danny answered without a lot of interest. "We were lucky enough to have horses, though we started out on bikes." She kept glancing around the room, rather than at him, and Russell found it quite irritating.

"Ah, I kept east of you, then, on Route 89. We?" Russell pressed, although he clearly didn't have her attention. "You weren't traveling alone."

"No, Danny was lucky enough to run into Tom," Melissa explained for her, when Danny didn't answer right away. "Tom Miller," Melissa added as if that should explain everything.

"I'm afraid I haven't been in Mercy long enough to know very many people," Russell said, offering Melissa a small but ineffective smile.

Danny finally focused on him again with a pained look. He suspected the journey wasn't something she normally chose to discuss, for understandable reasons. "My friend, Sam, and I came across Tom and his son in Idaho. His mom is Sandy Miller. They own Miller Ranch."

"Of course," Russell said with a quick nod of his head, though he'd known who Tom Miller was as soon as Melissa offered his name. He'd spent enough time listening to Patty drone on about him. "I heard Sandy's son had come home. I think I might have actually met him yesterday, although I never caught his last name. What a blessing."

Danny's eyes narrowed for a moment and Russell had to resist the temptation to squirm. How curious. He'd have to get to know her better.

"It's been nice meeting you," Danny said dismissively before shifting her attention back to the doctor. "I'll check in with you tomorrow and set up a time for us to get together. I need to go have Crissy introduce me to her and Chloe's friend."

"Oh, yes, that would be Trevor," Melissa laughed. "Do me a favor and make sure he doesn't get out of the wheelchair. Today is the first day I've let him out of bed and I'm concerned he's going to sneak off and undo all the work I did on his leg."

Russell looked past the women as they spoke and watched with some apprehension as a large golden retriever loped across the room. "Who let a dog in here?" he asked with contempt.

Danny frowned at him and Russell could feel his initial attraction for her turning to disdain. "That would be me," she said without any hint of contrition. "Her name's Grace. I thought she might be able to help lift some spirits. Isn't that something you approve of, Father?"

Russell understood then the level of Danny's intelligence, as well as her keen intuition. She was someone for him to avoid, not dance around with, and he was instantly annoyed with himself for not realizing it sooner. It proved how he was already getting too comfortable with his role in Mercy and was further evidence that his time to move on was quickly approaching. "I think that's a marvelous idea," he said to Danny without any inflection while backing away. Unfortunately, the dog followed him. As he turned around, Grace growled deep in her throat, and he quickly retreated without looking back.

Russell headed directly for the first-grade classroom that had been converted to a supply closet. His desire to spend the morning flirting with Melissa had soured, so he'd fold some sheets, stock some Band-Aids, and then find an excuse to leave early. Perhaps he'd take a stroll through town for inspiration. He wasn't sure yet how he was going to leave Mercy, though he had no doubt it would all be clear to him soon. The picture was already painted, he simply needed to stand back far enough to see it for what it was.

As he turned into the hallway, the sound of a man coughing drew his attention. Entering the front of the building was the councilman that Patty didn't get along with. Russell's unease from only moments before was instantly replaced with a confidence he was more familiar with. The vain man was easily manipulated, and he'd already considered seeking him out. They needed to talk.

"Gary, what are you doing here? I certainly hope you aren't ill."

Gary turned and attempted to wave off Russell's remark. "Thank you for your concern, Father, but it's only a head cold. I went to Mr. Sullivan's to get some over-the-counter medicine, and he told me Patty and the sheriff took it all from the store several days ago. I have to come here and get permission from Dr. Olsen to give me some."

Russell crossed his arms over his chest and tsked disapprovingly. "That seems rather excessively controlling, don't you think?"

Gary wiped at his nose and shrugged. "Maybe. Though I'm sure Dr. Olsen won't have any problem giving me a decongestant."

"That really isn't the point, is it?" Russell pressed, his face pinched with concern. "Oh, I suppose a councilman won't have any issues getting the medicine, and especially not the mayor.

But how about someone else? Say, an elderly woman who's been unable to carry water or bring food in for the market. Would she be turned away?"

Gary squirmed uncomfortably and glanced down the hall, toward the clinic area in the cafeteria. "I don't really see how that's relevant, Father."

Russell raised his eyebrows and looked down his nose at the man until Gary finally shifted his gaze to stare at his own feet in shame. "I feel it's quite relevant in light of the conversation I overheard yesterday."

This caused the reaction Russell expected, and the councilman jerked his head back up, his eyes widening slightly. "What conversation would that be?"

Russell first looked left and then right, to ensure that they were alone and to make Gary feel he was part of a privileged discussion. "I was collecting eulogies for Father White." Russell paused and swallowed hard, like he was overcome briefly by emotion before continuing. "I inadvertently heard Bishop and that new fellow in town, Tom, talking about something concerning with Sheriff Waters."

Gary's eyes narrowed. "What was it?"

Russell shook his head regretfully. "I wasn't going to say anything because gossip is the devil's language. However, I keep seeing more evidence of the power-hungry leaders of Mercy. I'm afraid there are those who want to take advantage of the genuine people such as yourself, Gary, and turn this into a dictatorship for their own gain. Even when that is at the cost of the safety and wellbeing of everyone else."

Gary blanched and took a firm grasp of Russell's arm, pulling him aside even though they were still alone in the hallway. "What are you talking about?"

"Were you aware that Patty intentionally misled our own

military into thinking Mercy is in quarantine?" Russell studied the other man's reaction. Interesting.

If he had to wager, he'd bet Gary already knew. Though he certainly didn't approve, so that was all that mattered. "She and her supporters have effectively cut your town off from any outside aid. All under the guise of a runaway military that's taking rather than giving."

"We've all heard the reports—"

"From what?" Russell challenged. "A Morse code message that her *husband* deciphered and reports from some scared riders on horseback? You need to remember that I was there for one of those attacks, Gary. That Pony Express rider wasn't attacked by our military. It was a teen boy and his starving friend."

Russell took a step closer to Gary and lowered his voice so that he was almost whispering. "I gave your mayor and Sheriff Waters a firsthand account of my own, personal interaction with the military I encountered. It wasn't far from here," he lied. "And the only thing they did was offer me food, first aid, and shelter."

"The council never heard anything about that," Gary stuttered, clearly flustered by the information. Russell was taking a chance by lying. However, if he was questioned, he had told Patty about his run-in with the army near the reservoir and that could easily be twisted around in his favor. It was easy to bend the truth, so long as a thin wisp of it existed to manipulate.

Russell shook his head in despair. "Don't you see? This is what I was afraid of! Information is power, Gary, and right now Patty has it all and is keeping the most important of it to herself."

Gary stepped back and coughed once, covering his mouth absently, his cold forgotten. "I've heard rumors and tried to confront Patty about them, but she either denied or defended her actions."

"Isn't there a council meeting in a couple of hours?" Russell prodded, cocking his head slightly to study the other man. "Maybe it's time you stepped up."

Looking rather shocked, Gary stumbled back out the front door, apparently forgetting his cold medicine. Russell smiled and followed him outside, deciding to forgo any more community service for the day.

CHAPTER 17

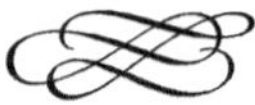

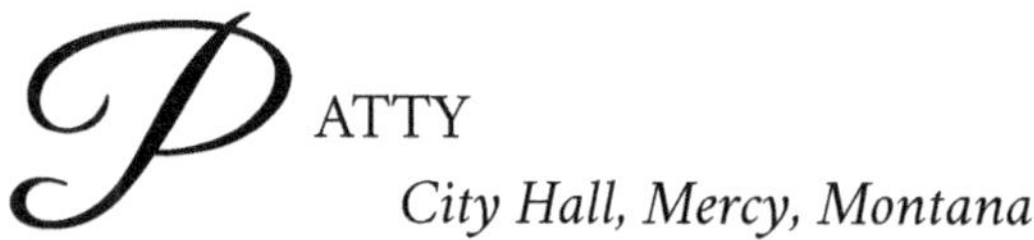

ATTY

City Hall, Mercy, Montana

PATTY COULDN'T REMEMBER the last time they'd had a council meeting during the day, and she'd gone around and opened all of the windows so that plenty of light poured into the room. An hour later she was regretting it as she sat squinting up at Tom while he finished what she was calling a "presentation" to the council and town leaders.

Patty had several reasons for starting the meeting off with Tom's personal account of their four-hundred-mile trek. Not only did it offer incredible insight into several facets of their societal breakdown, but it also revealed what was happening with the military. Her other motive wasn't as obvious and even Caleb didn't know what she was planning. A small smile tugged at Patty's mouth and she nodded silently to herself in approval. She had slept soundly the night before for the first time in three weeks. Sitting there, watching Tom as he held the room's occupants captivated, she knew she'd made the right decision.

"The day before we made it to the ranch was when we came across the desperados," he said solemnly. "Near the Miner's Trail, holed up in a small valley. I watched one of them slit Dan Erickson's throat, except I didn't know it was him at the time because his face had been mutilated."

There were small gasps from around the table and Patty's smile faded. She couldn't bear to look down at the far end, at Mr. Sullivan. Dan was his nephew, if Patty remembered correctly.

"What are we going to do about them?" Betty asked, her voice thick. The councilwoman looked scared, and Patty felt that was a good thing. It meant Tom was getting through to them about how precarious their situation was.

"A group of us have volunteered to go out as an armed escort with the next rider," Sheriff Waters answered. "We believe we know where they're being attacked, so we'll be ready for them."

"And if they aren't there?" Paul was the next to speak, and he kept glancing furtively beside him, at Gary. Patty suspected he already knew the answer.

"Then we'll go to them," Tom said, placing his hands palms-down on the table and leaning forward. "We stop them. Now, before they come to us."

Patty carefully observed the affirming head gestures and spoken words of support for the plan, stopping when she made eye contact with Gary. He wasn't joining in on the camaraderie and was instead staring at her with an open look of contempt.

"And by stop, you mean kill them?" Gary shouted, his words cutting through the murmurs and silencing the room.

Tom turned to the older man, his eyes narrowing. "I mean we'll do whatever it takes to keep Mercy safe."

"Whose decision was it to take our town to war?" Gary pushed. "I don't remember there being a discussion about it."

"Because there wasn't one," Sheriff Waters barked. "This is a security issue and since I'm in charge of security, Tom came to me, Gary. Anyone going is voluntarily doing it. You're welcome to join us."

That effectively shut the councilman up and Patty had to stifle a laugh, covering it by clapping her hands to redirect the groups attention. "I know Tom has given us a lot to think about and some of it might even make us question how we've been doing a few things, but right now we need to move on or else we'll be here all day. We still have several items of importance to discuss."

"I'm close to having my old motorcycle running," Al offered, raising a hand.

"Isn't that what you said at the last meeting?" Mr. Sullivan teased in an attempt to lighten the mood in spite of his family's loss.

Al scoffed good-naturedly. "The last couple of parts were lost with the riders who were…well, I mean to say that the parts were stolen. I'm hoping we can manage to get them replaced in the next week or two. The old truck is proving more difficult, since I had to yank out the whole wiring harness. There's ways to get around it all, of course," he added, scratching at his head. "Except we're nearly out of gas, so it doesn't much matter if I get anything running."

"Define 'almost out'," Bishop said, his concern obvious.

"After setting aside enough to run the generator at the clinic through the winter, we're down to around fifty gallons of diesel and less than a hundred of gasoline."

"We'll have to start scavenging the vehicles in town and then move on to any we find on the outer roads," Fire Chief Martinez suggested.

"Al has a valid point," Bishop said. "We might be better off focusing our energy and resources on things that we know will still be working a year from now."

"He's right," Sam added. "There won't be anyone producing new gasoline for a long time. Possibly never, so finding parts to build more wagons might be wiser."

When Patty saw more than one skeptical look, she stood and cleared her throat. "I know I briefly introduced Sam Ruiz, but I failed to mention he's a chemistry teacher, as well as extremely knowledgeable in several areas. He's already been a great help with suggestions to protect the spring water. He also has some ideas about indoor farming that I've asked him to share."

"I'm a chemistry teacher, not a botanist," Sam declared right away. "So, I'd like to start by saying that I need some volunteers to work with me on this project. Preferably people with some very green thumbs."

There was some scattered laughter, and a couple of hands went up in the air, including Betty. "I was born and raised on a working farm," she offered. "I don't know much about growing plants inside, but I do know a lot about plants in general."

"Excellent," Sam said happily. Looking at Paul, the other volunteer, he handed two sheets of paper to be passed down to him and Betty. "Here's a list of plants that grow well inside, according to the books I found at the school library yesterday and confirmed by Sandy Miller. We'll need to get together and come up with a master plan on how and where to best grow them, and we need to start soon. I'm sure everyone has noticed the acid rain is already having an impact on some of the more delicate foliage."

There were murmurs of agreement and Patty's stomach clenched as she thought about the browning leaves she'd seen on her apple trees that morning. How much more would they have to overcome?

"Growing some herbs and fruit in a bunch of greenhouses is one thing," Gary said, looking over the list Paul held out next to him. "But what are we going to do about the cattle? If the grasses and hay die off, so will the cows."

Sam glanced at Tom and then Patty, before clearing his throat. "Henry's Hollow."

Gary looked surprised, but Paul nodded his head. "Yes, that could work. Being indoors, so long as we keep it watered and get enough light in through the natural smokestacks, we should be able to get several harvests a year to make up for the lack in yield."

"You want to grow hay in a cave?" Al asked, perplexed. He rubbed at the stubble on his jaw and then shook his head. "I've never heard of such a thing."

"Indoor farming, and also what's called vertical farming, has been around for thousands of years," Sam explained. "It certainly isn't new, and from what I've been told, this cave might be a perfect opportunity. It's close enough to the spring that getting water in won't be impossible and the natural holes in the ceiling can be used to redirect the sunlight, in addition to possibly some solar panels and other options I'm still exploring."

"That old mine and cave is blocked off for a reason," Chief Martinez said, frowning. "I've been in there myself, and I'm telling you it'll be a lot of work to simply get it cleaned out. Then you'll have to haul tons of dirt inside, and that's after you come up with a way to safely move several crates of old, unstable dynamite."

"Dynamite?"

Patty had forgotten Russell was there, so she was surprised by the priest's question. Turning to him, she was curious about his reaction. He almost looked excited, rather than alarmed.

"And some of it's crystalized," Sheriff Waters added. "So, Chief Martinez is right. It's probably unstable."

"How many crates are we talking about?" Bishop asked, his face serious.

Chief Martinez shrugged. "I've got a detailed list somewhere at the station I can get for you. It's been a few years, but I want to say at least seven or eight. Those are fifty-pound boxes."

Bishop whistled. "That's an awful lot of unstable explosives."

The fire chief pursed his lips, looking irritated. "I've made two requests since I was hired to get a professional removal team in here. Gary shot it down each time, citing expense issues."

Gary shrugged. "I'm sure at the time it wasn't seen as a high priority. The material has been there for almost a hundred years without any problems."

"I read that a mosquito landing on it can set it off," Paul said, his eyes wide.

"That's a special derivative of nitroglycerin," Bishop corrected. "These old sticks are just straight-forward powdered nitroglycerin. If they've crystalized, then yeah, they'll go boom pretty easily, but it'll take more like a hammer strike than a mosquito," he added with a wink. "I've worked with it before on some of my jobs, so I'm sure we can safely remove it. We'll get to work on it as soon as we're back from the…ride."

"We'll need to slaughter the cow for the next barbeque in a couple of days," Patty said, trying to move the meeting along. "We learned last time that it takes longer than we expected. Tom has graciously agreed to continue to supply the town with the meat at our weekly dinners."

"If I'm not back by then, I've instructed Ethan on where to pull one from," Tom said. Pausing, he took a moment to look at everyone seated at the large table, as well Russell, who was leaning against the back wall again. "I want to make it clear that Miller Ranch will do everything in its power to help feed everyone in Mercy, but only if we're all in agreement that we can never force participation in the food exchange. And I'll never withhold food from someone who needs it, even if they haven't contributed."

Patty wished then that Sandy had come to the meeting. She would have been so proud of her son as everyone smiled at him in approval. However, Tom had explained that she, Chloe, and Ethan were busy working in the field cutting hay. He and Bishop needed to leave as soon as possible to get back and join them.

"Excuse me," Russell said, clearing his throat. "Mayor Patty asked me to attend so I could update you all on Father White's memorial service. It will be tomorrow evening, after dinner. I'm sorry that some of you will be gone and unable to attend," he said, looking pointedly at Tom, Bishop, and Sheriff Waters. "I've collected some lovely eulogies, though I imagined I would have more than three by now."

Patty wiggled guiltily in her seat. "I'm sorry, Father. I'll get mine to you this afternoon. Thank you for organizing it."

"Oh, you'll have to thank Madeline," Russell retorted, drawing some chuckles. "I'm simply doing her bidding at this point."

"We're running low on antibiotics again," Melissa said, when Patty motioned for her to talk. "The loss of our riders and the medicine they'd found for us was a huge blow. Hopefully we don't have any serious illnesses come up. Please remember that if you or anyone you know or see has obvious signs of something contagious, to take the proper precautions and let me know right away."

Gary chose that particular moment to cough and all eyes turned on him. Blushing, he wiped at his nose and then sat up defiantly in his seat. "It's a simple head cold," he argued. "And I wouldn't even have any symptoms if I'd been able to get some cold medicine," he directed accusingly at Patty.

"And that's somehow my fault?" she asked, finding his tone almost humorous.

"If it were only the medicine from Mr. Sullivan's that was taken, I wouldn't have such an issue with it," Gary retorted.

"Really, Gary?" Chief Martinez said, rolling his eyes. "We

made a group decision in the beginning to protect anything valuable in the store. I think any sort of medication qualifies."

"Perhaps," Gary agreed, his voice low. "How about the whole town?"

"What?" Betty asked, confused. "What do you mean by that?"

Patty exchanged a nervous look with Caleb. She'd been wondering how long Gary was going to sit on his suspicions and it looked like the time had come. She sighed, resigned to the situation. It didn't really matter anymore.

"Haven't any of you wondered," Gary was saying, "why, after three weeks, *and* with someone communicating with the outside world via a ham radio, we haven't had any direct contact with the military?"

"I think they're a little busy right now." Bishop's voice sounded dangerous and Patty knew she needed to preempt Gary and diffuse the situation.

Standing slowly, Patty took a step back from the table. "What Gary is trying to accuse me of, in a rather roundabout way, is that I made the decision to intentionally mislead the military into thinking we're still in a voluntary quarantine."

Patty raised her hands to silence the buzz of conversation as several people tried to ask her questions all at once. "It's true," she shouted, already feeling the weight lifting from her chest. "And while it turned out that I wasn't wrong, I could have been, and for that I am sorry."

"You're *sorry*?" Gary yelled, also rising. "You made the unilateral decision to cut us off from help when we need it most, and you're sorry?"

Caleb started to get out of his chair, but Patty stopped him with a light touch on his back. When he looked up at her, she simply smiled and shook her head once. She turned back to Gary. "Sit down."

The councilman stared at her, mouth open, and hesitated.

When he looked over at Paul for support, his friend remained silent. His face red, Gary made a show of slamming his hands on the table before doing as he was told and dropping back into his seat.

"You all know how much Mercy and the people in it mean to me," Patty said as she moved to the front of the room, next to the whiteboard. "We've all watched the numbers drop these past three weeks. Today, the only reason I'm not forced to change it again is because Tom and his friends came home."

Patty took a slow breath before stepping up behind Tom and setting her hands on his shoulders. "I'll stay on as a council-woman and be the same pain in the butt I've always been, but things have changed. The world has changed, and Mercy needs a different kind of leader. Effective immediately, I'm stepping down as mayor and I'm naming Thomas Miller the Interim Mayor of Mercy in my place."

CHAPTER 18

*D*ANNY
Mercy Fire Station, Mercy, Montana

DANNY STOOD HOLDING the fire helmet Chief Martinez handed her, fingering the dial in the back that adjusted the size. It was a habit she'd picked up during her initial training and never broke herself of. Most of the helmets were too big for her head, no matter how far down she dialed the inner meshing.

"I've got some gear that'll fit you," Chief Martinez was saying, continuing his recruitment attempt. It had been going for over an hour, ever since Danny arrived at the station. "Obviously not mine," he joked, in reference to his short stature.

Danny was a couple of inches taller than him, though he was built like a tank. "One of our volunteers was out of town when it went sideways and hasn't returned. He was tall and lanky," he added, gesturing to one of the open lockers where all the gear was stored. Danny picked up a jacket with the name Johnson stenciled on the back and tried it on.

"You're right, Chief," she said evenly. "It fits."

"Call me Carlos," the older man scoffed. "We're not formal around here."

Standing there in the bunker gear, surrounded by the tools she was familiar with and the smell of damp fire that always seemed to permeate every fire hall she'd been in, Danny felt at ease. Less than a month before she'd been desperate to get out, to run away from the responsibilities and weight of the memories. Something had changed during the four hundred miles of soul-searching. Danny wasn't sure if it was due to what was happening in the world around her, or if it was internal—it really didn't matter. "You can stop trying so hard," she laughed when Carlos approached her with a new pair of extrication gloves.

"Does that mean you'll join us?" he asked hopefully, eyebrows raised. Between his bushy mustache and wild brows, there wasn't much left of his face to see, though he was clearly smiling.

"It's in my blood," Danny said simply, knowing the career fireman would understand.

Nodding, Chief Martinez handed her the gloves and then walked to the open bay door. The early morning light offered a clear view of the interior, which housed two useless firetrucks. Some of the tools had been removed and were stacked on the floor around them for easy access. Danny's understanding was that they were still attempting to respond to emergencies from the building, and took turns keeping the station manned with at least two firefighters in addition to the chief, who was living there.

Grace was having a grand time, racing from item to item and sniffing it with intense interest. The chief didn't seem to mind and Danny imagined he'd be fine with making the retriever their mascot if it meant getting her on board. They were desperate for help and with Martinez being the only emergency medical technician, having a paramedic as part of the team was extremely appealing.

"We've got six volunteers," Martinez explained, turning from the sunlight to look at Danny. "Two of them are new since the flashpoint, so you can imagine how rough around the edges they still are."

Danny picked up one of the air packs and confirmed it was still working. She knew there wasn't anything electrical in them. It was all pressurized, including the regulator and gauge.

"The PASS device and low air alarms don't work, of course, but they're otherwise good as new," Carlos said, watching her examine the gear.

The PASS was a personal alert safety system that was normally tripped if there wasn't any movement for thirty seconds, or it could also be triggered manually by the firefighter if they were in danger. The thought of entering a fire without either alarm was disconcerting, although without a working firetruck or ability to charge a line, there really wouldn't be much need for the packs.

"I've been researching some of the old ways of fighting fires," Chief Martinez said, following her train of thought. "I've got some ideas I'd really like to run by you, when you have some time."

Danny set the pack down and then reached out to pet Grace when she ran up and slammed into her legs. "I've got some time commitments for the next few days, but I'll be back," she promised. "Meanwhile, how do we even know when there's an emergency?"

Unclipping a radio from his belt, Carlos handed it to Danny. "With only seven of these working right now, we're very limited. The mayor has one, Sheriff Waters, and Bishop for up at Miller Ranch. Then there's one at the clinic, the two checkpoints, and here at the station. So, most of the time it's still word-of-mouth. For that reason, we typically only respond to major incidents."

"For example?" Danny asked, curious.

"Well, like the wagon accident. They needed both our tools and manpower, as well as help to safely transport the survivors. Any accident where there's a substantial injury that requires boarding and properly securing the patient. Like the other day, we had a gentleman fall from a tree. Thankfully, Doc doesn't think he broke anything more than a bone in his foot, but we had some concern for his neck at first. I might not have the personnel right now for much more than basic first aid, other than myself, but I still have all the gear. I've been working on teaching everyone more basic life support, and even some ALS."

Advanced life support was usually reserved for paramedics and other health professionals, like nurses and doctors, but Danny could understand the need to extend the training to whoever was willing and able.

"We've been fortunate to have only had a couple of fires, after the initial ones were extinguished," the chief continued. "Obviously, any fires require all hands on deck plus anyone else we can recruit to carry water. We can still gear up and get in a lot closer than anyone else to try and extinguish it, but we're literally forming water brigades. That's something else I've been brainstorming on and would appreciate input from a seasoned firefighter."

"I heard church bells before when I was up at Miller Ranch," Danny said while thoughtfully tapping at her chin. "Could you use something like that instead of the klaxon? I imagine that blew out just like everything else." The alarm was often used in larger communities for rare occurrences like tornado warnings or tsunamis. Small communities still used them to call the volunteer firefighters to the station, instead of pagers.

"Yeah, its internal wiring basically melted into a blob," Carlos confirmed. "There was no salvaging it. The church bell isn't feasible because it's on the opposite end of town and up a few flights of steps. In a major incident it might make sense, but not for daily stuff."

Danny pivoted to study the vehicles behind them. One was an ancient tanker that had certainly seen better days, but the other was surprisingly newer-looking and appeared to be a decent rig. "How old is that?" she asked, pointing at the fire engine.

Carlos beamed, proud of his accomplishment even though it currently didn't work. "After 9/11 the federal government was handing out grants like candy. Mercy was still sitting on theirs when I got hired, so I completed the process and was able to pick up this almost-new engine."

Danny approached the bumper and confirmed her suspicions. Tapping the chrome device attached to it, she grinned at Chief Martinez. "Isn't this pneumatic?"

The chief tugged at his mustache for a moment as he thought about it until the implication sank in. Snapping his fingers, he immediately went to grab a toolbox. "Of course! I mean, it's hardwired into the truck, but I'm sure with a little work I can figure out how to manually activate it."

Danny chuckled as she watched the man begin to dismantle the alarm, and was tempted to stay and help him. Except she promised she wouldn't be gone for more than an hour. Without a watch she couldn't be sure, but by the time she rode back to the spring, Danny guessed it was going to be closer to two hours. Their goal was to finish the shelter by the end of the day and she was committed to seeing it through. "I really need to get going, Chief," she called out, unable to bring herself to call him by his first name. The man had been fire chief in Mercy for five years and had fifteen more years in the fire service in Spokane, Washington. It felt disrespectful not to recognize his position.

Tipping his hand in a mock salute while holding a wrench,

Martinez gave her a wink. "Understood. I'll be looking forward to seeing you around here next week, then. Meanwhile, you've already been a great help!"

Patting her thigh to call Grace, Danny headed out the bay doors. Squinting against the bright sunlight, she was surprised at how fast the day was heating up. It hadn't been that warm for a while and she hoped it was a good sign for the weather. Going to where her horse was tethered, she stopped when she recognized a white horse coming up the road. "Tom!" she called out, waving a hand at him.

Tom shifted in his saddle and smiled warmly when he saw her. Urging Lilly into a trot, they kicked up dust as they came towards her. Grace barked once and then began to wiggle in excitement. Danny wasn't sure if it was because of Tom or Lilly; the dog loved them both.

"Howdy, Mayor," Danny teased when he got close enough so she didn't have to shout.

Removing his cowboy hat, Tom chuckled while looking at her humbly. "How do you already know? It was news to me up until about an hour ago."

"Chief Martinez told me," Danny explained, tipping her head toward the fire station. "The title suits you," she added.

Tom dismounted in one fluid motion, landing just a few feet from her. Danny was instantly aware of his closeness and found herself drawn to him. Normally, she would have stepped back, but looking up at his sparkling green eyes and overgrown mop of black hair, she had to restrain herself from reaching out to touch his face.

"I'm not so sure about the title," Tom said, his voice softer than usual. "I tend to be a little impulsive. It might not be the best characteristic for a mayor."

"Don't worry," Danny offered, holding his gaze. "I'll be here to keep you in line."

Tom's eyes dropped momentarily to her lips and Danny's breath caught as he took a step towards her.

"Hey, Mr. Mayor!"

Tom's head jerked up as he sought out the source of the voice, and he lifted his hat to wave at a man riding by. "Hello, Eric!" he called back.

Danny tried to hide her disappointment as the spell, or whatever it was, broke and Tom moved closer to Lilly. He looked flustered and began tugging at the tack while attempting to make small talk. "You thinking of joining the fire department? Does that mean you'll be staying in Mercy?"

Feeling bold, Danny decided to continue with her apparent quest that day of taking leaps. Moving up next to Lilly, she reached up and put her hand on Tom's to stop his movements. "Yes, to both. And I'm glad I saw you, because I need to tell you that I won't be going tomorrow."

A rein still in his hand, Tom frowned at her. "Why not?" He must have realized how it sounded, because he rushed to cover up his initial response. "I mean, I'm relieved you've decided to stay. I'm just surprised because you were so...enthusiastic about it."

Danny laughed and moved to her own horse, thinking over how to respond. She'd rehearsed her speech countless times the night before, but now it seemed like it would be best to keep it simple and straight to the point. "As much as I want to see those guys stopped up close and personal, my place is here with my dad."

Danny was having a hard time gauging Tom's reaction. He didn't answer right away and his suddenly stoic demeanor reminded her of when they first met. The comparison was disturbing. Maybe she'd been wrong and his only interest in her was as a companion on the road or in a fight.

"I'm sorry," he said earnestly.

Danny had dropped her gaze to stare at Grace's ears while she rubbed them, and she looked up then, thrown off by both the words and his tone. Tom was staring at her intently. "Sorry for what?"

"For being selfish," he said. "With both you and Ethan. He's staying too, at the farm, which is where he should be. Just like you're right to stay with your dad. It's just that…I thought I'd have to force both of you to listen to reason. I don't know why my first reaction is to feel abandoned or something, because that doesn't even make any sense. I want you to stay here where you're safe."

Touched that he'd been so open about his feelings, Danny offered him an encouraging smile. "It makes total sense. We've all been through a lot and it feels wrong not to do it together." Sticking her foot in the stirrup, she mounted the horse, wishing she didn't have to get back to the spring.

Tom put his hat on and then smiled before leaping onto Lilly's back. "We're leaving early in the morning, so I need to get back to the farm and try to get some more hay harvested before we go."

"Crissy told me about the big hay cutting when I saw her at the clinic yesterday," Danny said. "Since we'll be done at the spring soon, would it be okay if I went and stayed out at the farm while you're gone? I can't replace you and Bishop, but I can pull my own weight."

"Ethan and Sam would really like that," Tom said, looking relieved. "And it would be good knowing you were there."

As Tom turned Lilly to face the other direction, Danny put a hand out to stop him. She waited until their eyes met before smiling playfully. "If it makes you feel any better, my first instinct *was* to go with you, Tom."

CHAPTER 19

*J*AMES
    Master Sergeant, US Marines, 1ˢᵗ Force Reconnaissance
Somewhere over Idaho

THE HELO PUT down in the small valley amid a whirlwind of dirt and debris, disturbing a small herd of elk in the process. James watched the massive beasts scatter, reminded of the numerous times he's been in similar landscapes with his father on annual hunting trips.

The hilly region of southern Idaho was rather desert-like, with lots of brown grass and tumbleweeds. The area around Boise, the capital, was full of plenty of ravines and low mountains that made it easy to find cover. Masking their arrival was still tricky, however, so they remained some distance away from the target. They'd wait until dusk and stay close to the hills to try and distort where the sound was coming from.

Their mission approach was to drop in from a safe distance

and hike for over four klicks to the property of the asset, Governor Alicia Jenson. Her estate was an impressive one hundred acres on top of one of the higher ranges that overlooked the city.

James had remained stoic while receiving his orders from General Montgomery the day before. Though he was disheartened to find the information they'd been slipped was true, he at least wasn't surprised by it. James feigned some hesitancy when the general initially handed him the directive, especially when it was followed by strict instructions not to inform his unit of any details until they were on site. It would have been abnormal for him to simply accept it too easily. What General Montgomery didn't realize was that James had already made the decision to not only disobey his command, but to commit what would likely be considered treason by the military leader. He wasn't going to bring the governor back to him.

"Lieutenant Carpenter," James barked once the engine had wound down, turning to face the pilot.

"Yes, sir?" the young officer replied hesitantly. Lucas was right that James didn't address the man very often. He wasn't sure why, except that the lieutenant hadn't been a part of their team prior to the flashpoint, so he didn't automatically include him in their conversations. However, Jeff had been through some hairy situations and never let them down. James was counting on their brief but intense history to sway the guy's loyalty.

"You've familiarized yourself with the secondary EXFIL?"

"Sure, Sarge," Carpenter replied without any hesitation. "Plenty of room in the back field, although I hope we don't have to use it. We'd all pretty much be sitting ducks."

James pulled his headset down around his neck and then rubbed at his jaw. "Change of plans. That's now our primary INFIL."

The lieutenant blinked a couple of times before glancing over at Lucas and the other guys seated around the cabin. "I don't understand. I thought our orders were to—"

"Your orders now are to drop us off in that field at dusk, Lieutenant. Will that be a problem for you?" James continued to stare at the other man, his steely gaze unwavering. He knew he was intimidating and he normally didn't go out of his way to take advantage of it, but their current situation called for extreme measures.

Lieutenant Carpenter balked, his color notably lightening a few shades. "No, uh…sir, it's just that—well, you're all likely to meet some heavy resistance if we announce ourselves like that."

"Does the loudspeaker on this bird work?" James asked.

Carpenter nodded and then glanced again at Lucas.

"Don't sweat it, man," Lucas reassured him. "We're gonna sweet-talk our way inside. Sarge has a way with words, you know?"

The lieutenant didn't look comforted as he turned back to James. "May I ask why we're choosing such an exposed entry, sir?"

"The mission parameters have changed," James said without looking at the rest of the men on his team. He'd already briefed the other three before leaving. He decided to tell them everything, and let them decide on their own if they wanted to be involved or pull out. All five men were seated behind James, and he believed the pilot would agree to his orders since the rest of the 1st Recon Unit were standing in solidarity. At least, he hoped so, or else they were pretty much screwed.

"We need you to fly this bird so we can make sure the asset is safe," Jay added, leaning forward. "Our goal here hasn't changed, except that we're trying to do it without any casualties."

James had debated for a few hours whether to stick to the original mission plan or deviate from it. In the end, it came down to proving to the governor that they were there to help her.

Killing off her security, staff, and possibly friends or family wouldn't be a good way to start the relationship. They'd been given access codes to the house alarm system that had been jury-rigged, but while that might get them in the house undetected, there wouldn't be any way around leaving a mess in their wake once inside.

Instead, James was going with a direct approach. Alicia Jenson was a seasoned US governor. A military helicopter coming in nice and slow in to her backyard, announcing its peaceful intentions without any fireworks might just work. At least, James was banking on it. It might be the only way to meet with her and get an opportunity to convince her she was in danger. Any further plans wouldn't work unless they had her cooperation and that couldn't happen if she was a hostage.

According to Lucas, Lieutenant Carpenter was a sharp guy and James could tell the man was putting some of the pieces together. After all, he was the reason they knew about the admiral. Nodding, the pilot shifted in his seat and slapped at a few switches on his control panel. "I'm on board, Sarge. We'll need to lift off in a few minutes and I'll bring her in low and hot until the final couple of klicks. The control for the external speaker is over there," he added, pointing to where the handset was clipped. "She's a bit touchy so be sure to press that button down nice and tight."

Less than half an hour later, the sun was slipping below the horizon to their backs as they hovered over the expansive property of the Jenson estate. Idaho was one of the few states that didn't have a governor's mansion and James considered it a great piece of luck. Otherwise, instead of being high in the hills on the outskirts of town, they'd have to penetrate deep into the large city of Boise.

Sweat trickled down James's neck as he held the handset to his mouth. He was normally extremely confident when executing missions, and he didn't like the feeling of unease pressing against his chest. "This is Master Sergeant James Campbell of the US Marines 1st Force Reconnaissance. We are here on a peaceful diplomatic mission and request to meet with Governor Jenson."

James leaned his head in Jay's direction, which was enough to elicit the information he wanted. "I've got five tangos in view, Sarge. All hot."

"None of 'em are firing yet, so there is that," Lucas added from his perch near the open door in the cabin. The white-knuckle grip on his M4 Carbine was the only evidence of his nerves.

"I've got movement!" Corporal Flores shouted. He was staring through his night-vision goggles and dropped to his stomach to get a more solid view with less movement.

"One more tango at the back door," Jay confirmed. "And… your charming personality must have done the job, Sarge. They've lowered their weapons to a ready position."

"Bring us in," James said stoically. There was a flurry of movement behind him as his men fell into position. He knew he didn't need to look to make sure they were in the proper formation.

As the helo touched down, he was the first to step off, and the first to reach who he was assuming was the head of the governor's security. He was a tall, middle-aged man in a black suit without any insignia and he didn't look happy.

"Nathan Hawk," the man said, extending a hand.

James was acutely aware of the five other men in view, all armed with automatic rifles. It was difficult to tell in the dark, but their uniforms looked like National Guard. That was good. "Sergeant Campbell," he replied, taking Nathan's hand in a solid grip.

"This is highly unusual," Nathan admonished, dropping James' hand. "So I'm sure you can understand why Governor Jenson isn't all that eager to grant you an audience."

"I understand," James said, his words sharp. "I'll be blunt. We were sent here to kill you and take the governor by force. Instead, we'd like to help protect her."

Nathan Hawk took a step back and carefully studied each of the four soldiers, then the helicopter, where the other two were perched in the doorway. James suspected the guy was ex-military, so he'd know what the 1st Force Recon team was. He'd also know that meant the five men he had out in the yard wouldn't be enough, and if he wanted to avoid a bloodbath, Hawk's only option was to trust him.

"Come this way," Hawk finally said as he turned around abruptly and waved a hand.

James motioned with two fingers, prompting Jay and Lucas to fall in behind him, while Corporal Flores remained at the edge of the lawn.

While the house wouldn't necessarily qualify as a mansion, it was certainly impressive. The three floors of living space had to add up to at least five thousand square feet, and it took a couple minutes before they reached a large, inner den on the top floor.

Seated on a couch in front of a roaring fire was a petite woman dressed in jeans and a sweatshirt. She held what looked like a glass of whiskey and had a perturbed look on her older, yet attractive face. "I assume you have a compelling story to tell me."

James stopped just past the threshold of the room, and with a small nod of his head left Lucas at the door, while Jay followed him inside. "I wish you were wrong," he said in response, which elicited a smile from the governor.

"My God, you're a large man," she said in amazement. "And you don't look like regular military."

"No, Governor Jenson. I'm Master Sergeant Campbell, and I run a special ops team in the Marines called the—"

"1st Force Reconnaissance," the governor finished for him. "I was a military brat," she explained, lifting her glass. "I recognize your patch. Now, let's skip the rest of the pleasantries, shall we?

First of all, I'm a senator now. I made that official a couple of days ago, but I imagine General Montgomery hasn't gone out of his way to spread the announcement."

So the plan was already in motion, James realized. Lucas had been right and it only confirmed he'd made the right decision to abort the original mission. "First of all, you have a mole on your staff," he said without any more preamble. Stepping forward, he removed a folded sheet of paper from a front pocket on his vest and handed it to her without further comment.

It took the senator all of ten seconds to figure out what the numbers were and what it meant. "Nathan," she snapped. He rushed to look at it for himself, and his face clouded.

"I updated these codes myself four days ago," he insisted.

James idly wondered how they'd managed to get a working system set up. Based on all of the lights burning, they obviously had at least one good generator operating. It was impressive, but he didn't have time to ask questions about it. They needed to get moving.

"General Montgomery has targeted you," James said. That got her attention and she set her glass down on a table abruptly, spilling some of the liquid. "I have reason to believe that Vice Admiral Baker was already assassinated. You're a threat to him, Senator."

"You were sent here to kill me?" she gasped.

"Not directly," he explained. "Our mission was to bring you back, based on your name being on the Survivor's List."

"The Survivor's List?" the senator snorted. "I thought that was a myth."

"It's not," James said without any humor. "I don't know if you're really on it or if it was just an excuse, but for whatever reason, the general wants you alive. We were sent here to get you...at any cost."

Senator Jenson stood abruptly, her nostrils flaring. "It's

because he knows I have too many followers. If he kills me outright, it will incite others to take up my cause. But this? Proclaiming me to be some sort of asset and taking me into false protective custody…" Her words trailed off as she began to pace the room, trying to put it together. "I'm sure he's got a plan to coerce me somehow."

"Where's your family?" James asked, glancing at Hawk. He wasn't sure of the man but the senator obviously trusted him.

"Already hidden," she said quickly, and then paused. "You don't think…"

"Come with us." They were out of time and James didn't have any other choice than being direct. "We'll protect you and eventually get you and your family to a safe place, if possible."

"Why?" the senator asked. Although clearly terrified, she still stood straight and held her chin high. "Why go against orders and risk everything for something you don't even understand?"

"Because this is personal for me." James took another step closer so the senator would be sure to see his face and hopefully be convinced he was telling her the truth. "My father is on the list. Somehow, Montgomery seemed to know that. Or he at least suspected it, and I believe that was why he chose my recon team to retrieve it, when he learned we were close by after the gamma ray hit. The general thought he could use my father as a way to manipulate me and guarantee my allegiance."

Senator Jenson stared at him for a moment before a small smile played at her lips. "Well, that seems to have backfired."

"I'm a soldier, Senator. But my loyalty is to the government, not any one man."

"If Montgomery's got a spy here, then we'll need to make it look like you were taken by force," Hawk said, surprising James.

"It might buy us a day or two before he starts actively looking for us," James offered.

Senator Alicia Jenson put both hands on top of her head,

entwining her fingers in her thick black hair she'd piled up in a messy bun. She looked younger than her years, even vulnerable for a brief moment, until she took an audible breath and gathered herself. "Okay. Give me five minutes," she said as she headed for a door at the back of the room.

Ten minutes later, the four of them made their way silently back the way they'd come. As they approached the doors at the rear of the house, James easily picked the small woman up and she pretended to struggle vainly against his thick arms, a muffled scream working its way around his hand that was clamped gently over her mouth. Jay held his Glock to the back of Nathan Hawk's head and the man walked stiffly outside with his hands out in front of him. Lucas brought up the rear, holding his rifle at the ready on all of them.

"Drop your weapons!" Nathan shouted to the men surrounding the helicopter. "Do it, or they'll kill the senator!"

There was one long, very tense moment as the five National Guard soldiers debated the order given to them by a civilian security guard. "Please do what they want!" the senator shouted as James conveniently moved his hand to the side.

Flores was joined on the grass by Corporal Lance and Sergeant Lee, and the additional firepower was enough to convince the guardsmen to listen to the senator. Not waiting for a better opportunity, James led the way, running across the open space while cradling the woman he'd promised to protect in his arms. Just as he reached the open door of the helo and set her inside, shots rang out.

Spinning around, James watched as Nathan went down, throwing Jay off balance and leaving them both vulnerable. His M4 was in his hands before James even completed the thought to reach for the rifle, and he directed a short burst of rounds towards their assailant. His aim was true and the uniformed man jerked several times before crumpling to the ground.

Lucas and Flores were already dragging the other two men the rest of the way and they were all in the helo by the time the original guardsmen had reacted and retrieved their weapons. Some random shots hit harmlessly off the underside of the bird, but the sharp retorts were enough to point out how close they'd come to complete failure.

"I'm okay," Hawk was shouting to the senator, who was urgently trying to get a good look at the bullet wound in the man's lower leg.

Flores made quick work of Nathan's pants and then used their field kit to clean the oozing hole. "He's right," he said after only a couple of minutes. "Went through and through. I doubt it impacted the bone. We'll get him patched up and as good as new."

"Who was that?" James demanded, ignoring the injury.

"He was assigned earlier this week by the Army," the senator explained.

"He was supposed to be out at the front gate," Hawk added. "I already suspected he was the mole, and this pretty much confirms it. He was either trying to prevent you from taking me with the governor, so she'd be alone, or else he saw through our charade."

"Doesn't really matter," Jay said. "He won't be talking to anyone."

"Where are we going?" Senator Jenson asked. Her hands were covered in blood and she looked more like a wild pioneer fresh from battle than a US Senator.

James glanced first at each of his men, before settling on the senator's scared but hardened features. "We were sent to get you because you're a threat," he said evenly. "For whatever reason, General Montgomery believes my father is a threat, too. It's time to find out why."

CHAPTER 20

ETHAN

Miller Ranch, Mercy, Montana

ETHAN LEANED against the long wooden handle of the sickle and stared out over the field of billowing hay. The sun was about to set and was casting one of its incredibly colorful sunsets throughout the valley spread below them. It had been a warm day and the birds were out late, taking advantage of the early evening insects hovering over the tall grasses. While it was a mesmerizing view, and one Ethan would have been in awe of at any other time in his life, it instead caused a heavy sense of foreboding.

The colors of the sunset were wrong, the grass was too brown, and the birds' flight patterns still often erratic. Although the sky was several shades away from night, the northern lights were already active, throwing additional shadows and hues into the increasingly unearthly landscape.

"It doesn't seem right that it should look so beautiful," Chloe said, moving up next to him.

He glanced over at her and marveled again at how someone so small could contain so much energy and strength. She'd kept up with him the whole day, and while she might not be able to swing a sickle in as wide a span, she certainly held her own. Ethan knew she probably understood why the scene bothered him, and she'd pretty much nailed it. "Yeah," he agreed. "The destruction of the Earth should be…less colorful."

Chloe snorted and then punched him in the arm.

"Ouch!" he quipped, rubbing at his shoulder only half-jokingly.

"Breaktime's over, Romeo. Sam just got here so he's going to help Crissy and Sandy haul the last of the bales over to the barn." Chloe raised the sickle over her head and made a ridiculous calling noise like a Jawa creature from *Star Wars*.

Laughing, Ethan joined her, and together they sprinted back to the last row they'd started cutting, sounding like two lunatics who had lost their minds.

Fifteen minutes later, his dad rode up on Lilly and called out a loud greeting to prevent any accidental hacking. Ethan and Chloe were long past their playfulness and back into a steady cadence of swinging and sweating to an internal rhythm. Sucking in a breath of dusty air, Ethan wiped at his forehead as he looked up at his dad.

"It's long past quitting time," Tom said, his face in shadows. The last of the sun's rays were barely reaching up from behind the mountains to the west and they were probably getting more illumination from the northern lights. "You must be starving."

"Famished," Chloe answered. Stretching her back, she squinted over to where Bishop was still tying up another bundle of hay. "You guys about done?"

Tom tipped his hat back and shifted in the saddle, the leather creaking under his weight. "We're calling that the last bale, so why don't you head back to the house and get the fire going? Throw some of those fish on to cook that you caught this morning, Ethan. Crissy said there was a good batch of eggs today so we can cook up some omelets, too."

"We'll wait for Sam to cook the omelets," Ethan said. "He's the only one who can make 'em good, except for Grandma."

"Crissy and your grandma are in the barn using the horses to arrange the bales," Tom explained. "It's like a giant jigsaw puzzle."

"Perfect," Chloe laughed. "Crissy loves puzzles. Come on," she said, grabbing at Ethan's arm and already pulling him down the hill.

"Tell Sam to hurry up," Ethan called to his dad as they marched away. The older man had been working at the spring with Danny for most of the day. His arrival probably meant that they'd all finished the water shelter, which was a good thing. Ethan was eager to talk with him about it, and to find out how the council meeting that morning went. All he got out of his dad before he started working was the shocking news that he was now the interim mayor of Mercy. Which was cool and everything, but he also wanted to know what they'd said about the cave and indoor farming.

The hay field sat on a hill to the southeast and wasn't too far from the house. The barn was in the opposite direction, so Ethan and Chloe opted to carry the tools back with them to the farmhouse, rather than go the extra distance. Resting the sickle in the crook of his arm as they walked, Ethan gingerly removed his work gloves, exposing several blisters.

Chloe glanced over and wrinkled her nose. "I'm afraid to take mine off without being close to some cold water and a bottle of numbing Bactine. I'm pretty sure I've got blisters on top of blisters."

"With Dad and Bishop taking off tomorrow morning, it's only

going to get harder," Ethan said, already regretting exposing his open wounds to the air. He decided it would hurt more to pull the gloves back on, so he stuffed them into the back pocket of his dirty jeans and slung the blade over his shoulder.

"Are you worried about them?" Chloe asked. She sounded much less sarcastic than usual.

Ethan scratched at a new mosquito bite on his forehead. It was ironic that of all the things in the world, the annoying insect thrived in the wake of the radiation. He shrugged in response, but then realized Chloe probably couldn't see him. It was almost dark. "I guess so. I mean, those outlaws are pretty dangerous, but I don't think they stand much of a chance against us. Sheriff Waters worked as a cop in a big city for a long time, and some of the guys who volunteered to go are veterans and good at handling guns. I don't know much about Bishop, but my dad is… well, he's my dad. He can be kinda scary when he's mad."

"So can Bishop," Chloe said quietly.

Ethan looked sideways at her, unsure by what she meant. "How so?"

She was using her sickle like a walking stick, and Ethan was distracted by how stunning Chloe looked in the gathering darkness. There was just enough purple left in her short, dark hair to make it stand out in the fading light, and there was something about the way she held herself; a confidence he was drawn to. He felt stronger when he was around her.

"You heard about how that kid Jason and his goons tried to attack me and your grandma up at the lake?" she asked, her eyes widening at the memory and flashing in the light cast on them now from overhead.

Ethan tried to ignore the intensity of the northern lights and instead focused on Chloe. "Yeah, I heard. Grandma said Bishop disarmed one of the guys, so I assume he can hold his own in a fight."

Shaking her head, Chloe's brows pinched together in a pained expression. "Yeah, something like that."

"I guess that means he'll be someone good to have there tomorrow," Ethan offered, not sure what else to say. "Dad said Danny's going to come stay with us while he's gone."

"Good. We can use all the help we can get if we ever want to finish cutting all of that hay," Chloe sighed. "I sure hope those cows appreciate it."

"*We'll* appreciate it when we're still eating beef next year," Ethan laughed, then stopped when he realized what he said. "I mean, you'll probably be gone by then. You know, with your parents back in Washington."

Chloe's steps faltered slightly and Ethan rolled his eyes at himself, thankful it was dark enough that she couldn't see him. "Caleb will find them," he offered lamely.

"He's still trying," Chloe said after a brief hesitation. "I don't know when it'll be, but someday I'll find out where they are, and if they're still alive."

"They are," Ethan insisted, and reached out in the dark to find her hand. He was relieved when instead of pulling away, she grasped his back, even though it made his blisters burn.

"When are you going to take me to see Henry's Hollow?" Chloe said, lightening the tone. She swung his hand back and forth like they were Hansel and Gretel on their way back to their house. It was hard not to play along.

"I guess I do owe you," Ethan said, lengthening his stride to keep up with her short, quick steps. "If we get enough done in the field tomorrow, maybe the next day we can take an extra-long lunch break and take a ride over there. I want to check out the new shelter anyway."

"It's a date," Chloe said, and squeezed his hand a little tighter. After a moment, she slowed and pulled his arm back, forcing him to stop. He turned expectantly to her, and was surprised when he saw how serious her expression was. "I'm glad you're not going tomorrow." Moving the sickle to her other side, Chloe stepped in closer to him so he could see her face. "I'd be super worried about you."

Ethan smiled. For the first time in what was only weeks but felt like a lifetime, he didn't have a heavy weight pushing him into the ground. Relief flooded him, prompted by the knowledge that he would be okay. With the love of his family and new friends, he would have the strength to combat the oppressing anxiety he'd been suffering. He knew he still had the capacity to feel alive and experience something that seemed impossible just days before. Joy.

CHAPTER 21

Miller Ranch, Mercy, Montana

TOM WAS RESISTING the urge to make some coffee, especially since it meant stoking the fire back up in the kitchen. It was already too hot inside the house. As he approached the kitchen while continuing the internal debate with himself, he saw that there was already a candle burning, and his mom was sitting at the counter, mug in hand.

"Can't sleep?" he asked, sliding onto the stool next to her. Based on the lack of enticing aroma, he guessed she was drinking tea.

"I thought I'd sleep better once you were back," Sandy said softly, swirling the contents of the half-empty cup. "I just can't seem to get my mind to shut off once I've closed my eyes. And it's so damn dark."

Tom put an arm around his mother's shoulders and noticed for the first time how much weight she'd lost. She was never what he'd call overweight, but rather sturdy. He couldn't ever remember feeling her bones poke through her robe the way they were now. It made Tom want to protect her even more, and he lightened his grip, afraid he was going to hurt her. "Things will get better," he said reassuringly. He wanted to promise her and opened his mouth to say the words, but he'd seen too much. Making a promise his mom knew Tom couldn't keep wouldn't help, and it wouldn't make the darkness go away or the power come on.

Standing, Sandy slid out from under her son's arm and began going through the motions of making him a cup of tea. "You know, your father almost ran for mayor once, a few years before he got sick."

Tom didn't try to hide his surprise. "Dad? Run for office? I never took him for much of a politician. I don't know how many times, or different variations, I heard of the story when he got in the fight with one of the councilmen during an open meeting in city hall."

Sandy scoffed as she poured the tea. "That was a long time ago, and Ed had it comin'. He would have won had he run. Only reason he didn't was because Ned decided at the last minute to serve for one more term, so he pulled his hat out of the race."

Tom took the steaming cup from his mom and smiled in disbelief. "Huh, I guess maybe Patty isn't totally crazy after all."

"Oh, Patty is crazy, all right," Sandy laughed. Finishing the last sip in her cup, she took it to the sink and rinsed it out with the remaining hot water from the kettle before turning back to Tom. "Except she was right about you. You're going to make a wonderful mayor, Thomas. I encouraged your dad to run again when Ned retired, but he was already sick by then. That was when you were living in Helena."

"I'm sorry," Tom said automatically.

"No," Sandy urged, moving back to him and clasping both of

his hands. "Don't ever be sorry for going out into the world and finding yourself and living your own life. We all have to at some point unless we want to live with resentment and wondering what might have been. I'm just so happy you came home to Mercy. Not once, but twice now. When we've needed you most, you're here, and now the town needs you, too."

Standing, Tom pulled his mom in for a familiar, comforting embrace. "I'll come back again, Mom." he added, feeling confident enough to make that particular oath.

Nodding, Sandy pulled back and tried to avert her watery eyes. "You should get to bed now. You and Bishop have a long ride ahead of you tomorrow."

Tom grinned at his mom, knowing better than to argue with her. "Yes, Mom. Just as soon as I finish going over a few things with Bishop. Goodnight," he said as she walked down the hall, grateful to be back at Miller Ranch.

A few minutes later, he knocked on the bunkhouse door when he saw there was still some light spilling out through the curtained window. Sam answered it fast enough to indicate he hadn't been in bed, and Tom nearly laughed when he saw the older man in his boxers. He was holding a notebook covered in writing, and his thick head of hair stuck up haphazardly in several directions. He looked like a crazed professor.

"Tom!" Sam said with some surprise. "Thought you were Bishop and was wondering why in the world he'd be knocking."

"What are you working on?" Tom asked, unable to make much sense of the scribbled words on the paper.

"Oh! Just doing some more research into the different indoor growth methods, including hydroponics and terracing. It's pretty fascinating stuff and I think there's much more potential than we realize. The hardest part might be coming up with enough healthy seeds."

Tom blinked at him a couple of times. "Okay…"

"Well Tom, you *are* Mayor Miller now, so perhaps that's something you could look into, or get on a list somewhere," Sam said, unable to contain his laughter at Tom's expression.

Tom rolled his eyes at the cheap joke. "Sure, Sam. As soon as you fill out a form to make an official request."

"Seriously, though," Sam said quickly, tossing the notebook onto one of the beds behind him. "I think it's great Patty named you mayor. There's no doubt you're the right person for the job. I'm just sorry I'm not going with you guys in the morning. Doesn't feel right to stay behind."

Tom started to reach out to pat Sam's arm to reassure him, and hesitated when he realized the other man was still dressed in only his underwear. "We'll definitely miss you," he said, opting to rest his hand on the doorframe and lean against it. "Better to stay here, though, than to suffer the wrath of Dr. Olsen. Neither one of us would ever hear the end of it, from both her and Danny."

"I'm sure to catch some grief from Danny tomorrow when she sees me in the dusty hay field," Sam complained. "I don't think I'll ever be able to convince her that my lungs are healed."

Tom scratched at his head and then peeked past Sam to confirm the room was empty. "As much as I like talking to you when you're half-naked, I was looking for Bishop. Know where he is?"

Sam gestured to the building behind them. "I think that man hardly sleeps. He's in there working on the wagon. See you in the morning," he added as Tom gave a small wave and headed for the barn.

The interior was dimly lit by only one oil lamp hanging on a center peg, though it was enough for Tom to see that the main area of the barn was empty. The wagon wheel Bishop was working on was propped on a couple of sawhorses and there were tools on the ground near it, but no sign of the engineer.

Tom moved to the center of the barn and was about to call

out for him when something made him hesitate. A sound that was off, maybe, or just a sense that he wasn't alone with the horses. Standing there, Tom held his breath and tilted his head, listening.

There. The creaking of a board above him. Pivoting, Tom studied the underside of the floor that made up the loft area of the old barn. The forward section was still used for storing excess hay, and the back half was closed off. It used to serve as the original bunkhouse until Tom built the new, larger one. For the last few years the useless space housed boxes of old tax forms and other unwanted items.

As he moved to the base of the ladder, Tom heard another, unmistakable sound of someone moving around in the room. Frowning, he began to quietly climb the ladder. Bishop exploring the barn in itself wasn't that odd. It was because he was doing it in the dead of the night that Tom got curious. And something else...instinct, told him it was because he was doing something he didn't want anyone to know about. For that reason, Tom had every intention of seeing what it was, unannounced if possible.

The original wooden ladder had broken on him the last time he carried a box up it, and nearly caused Tom to take a nasty spill. That meant the one there now was new enough that it made hardly any noise as he made his way to the top. Once there, Tom hoisted himself through the opening in the floor and crouched, listening. There was an odd tapping noise that he hadn't heard from below and a light spilled across the floor through the open door.

Standing, it took Tom four quick, long strides to cross the space and enter the room. He took the scene in rapidly and reacted without even thinking. A lantern was on the floor, while Bishop sat at an old desk with a headset on and what looked like a large ham radio in front of him. He'd been drumming out a message, to whom Tom couldn't guess, and his hand was poised with a pencil over a notebook.

As Bishop stood and turned to face him, his face a mix of shock and anger, Tom was already on him. Grabbing the other man by the front of his shirt, Tom hauled him the rest of the way to his feet and slammed him up against the nearest wall. "What is this?" he demanded, shaking Bishop once for emphasis.

"What's the matter with you?" Bishop retorted, not making any attempt to push back. "Caleb's been teaching me how to use the radio. I'm just practicing."

Tom's fury wavered, and he wondered if maybe the current situation was a prime example of why he wasn't mayor material. Was it possible he jumped to the wrong conclusion? Then, he caught the older man's eyes flitting to the desk and back to Tom again. Turning his head, Tom saw that Bishop had been in the middle of writing something when he'd interrupted. There were several sheets of paper, but the top one was all that mattered to him. In bold letters was a word he recognized, followed by a confusing set of statements:

MERCY. Will add to list. Unknown survival at this point. Still looking. Information sent to government agencies. Military status questionable. Be careful.

Tom's eyes narrowed as he re-read the words, taking into consideration that these were the *responses* back to Bishop that he had written down. The implication became vividly clear and he slammed his fist on the desk, scattering the rest of the papers onto the floor.

"Tom," Bishop said cautiously, holding a hand out. "It's not what you think."

Tom knew when he was being lied to. He always had. It was a knack he'd picked up as a teen and it had served him well in life. He'd been trying to deny the feeling about Bishop since they'd first met. Tom wanted to like the guy. He wanted to trust him, because his mom did, but there was something about him that didn't ring true. Bishop was lying and now Tom knew it had something to do with the military. He was putting Mercy at risk.

Scowling, he reached for Bishop again with the intent of making sure he left the farm, physically if he had to. Tom was a couple of inches taller than the other man and while Bishop was obviously tough, he also had close to twenty years on Tom so he shouldn't be much of a physical threat.

To Tom's shock, he never completed the motion. Bishop moved with lightning speed, grabbing Tom's hand and twisting it around and then up behind his back, forcing Tom to move with him or else risk breaking his arm. Bishop slammed into his back and used the combined force of their momentum to carry them both to the floor. Before Tom could offer any resistance, Bishop was on him, controlling his other arm with a knee across his shoulders and pressing his face into the rough boards of the floor.

"I don't want to hurt you," Bishop growled, close to Tom's ear. "So stop acting like a hotheaded fool."

Stunned, Tom gulped in a breath of dusty air and accepted the fact he'd been easily beaten by a fifty-something pencil pusher from Butte, Montana. Coughing once, Tom remained still, but he didn't relax and kept the tension against both Bishop's grip and the knee at his neck. "Who are you?" he demanded.

Bishop snorted once and then the weight disappeared from Tom's back. "If I let you up, can we act like men and have a conversation?"

Tom nodded once, his nose bent at a painful angle, and then slowly pushed himself into a seated position when Bishop released his arm. It was the same shoulder that had been shot, and Tom rolled it slowly to stop the spasm he was suffering.

"I'm sorry if I hurt you," Bishop offered. "But you didn't give me much choice."

Irritated by what Tom took as arrogance, he grunted as he forced himself to his feet so he could face the other man. "You act like you have rights here. This is *my* home and my town, and you're the one threatening it!" he shouted, pointing a finger at Bishop's chest. "You don't get any choices, Bishop. You either explain to me what the hell is going on, or you get out!"

Bishop stared at him silently and Tom braced himself to kiss the floor again. He might be older and smaller, but the man knew how to fight.

"I respect you," Bishop said evenly. "And I care about your mother—"

"You leave my mom out of this!" Tom's temper flared and he almost forgot about the splinters in his face.

Holding a hand up defensively, Bishop then motioned for Tom to settle down. "I don't know what you think I'm doing up here, but if you look at the other pages on the ground, it might help shed some light."

Tom begrudgingly bent over and snagged two sheets that were by his feet. They were full of the same tight script as the other one and had choppy, unfinished sentences:

Washington communication sketchy. Focusing on eastern region where Chloe is from. Southern California no contact yet. Will keep trying. Contact with Honolulu. Waiting on names.

Tom frowned and looked up at Bishop, who was watching him closely. "I have a good friend who happens to be in charge of the Washington State Guard," Bishop explained. "I finally made contact with him a couple of days ago and he's helping me try to find the kid's parents. And hopefully Ethan's mom."

"Whose radio is this?" Tom asked, unsatisfied.

Pushing away from the wall, Bishop retrieved the headset from the floor and went to examine the radio to make sure it was still working. "This was Caleb's main radio. It got fried the day of the gamma ray. Well, it was mainly the battery that got fried and only some of the electrical circuits. I offered to try and fix it for him."

"He showed me his other radio," Tom said, eyes narrowing. "He specifically said it was the only working radio in Mercy, and that the other nearest one he knew of was at the Pony Express station near Helena."

Bishop dropped the headphones on the desk and turned abruptly to face Tom. He looked annoyed, but also resigned. "That's because I didn't tell him I got it working. I knew how everyone would react to my wanting to contact the state guard." He rushed to explain when Tom bristled. "And you're right, Tom. I haven't been upfront with everyone regarding my background. I was in the military and I still have some contacts. I've been using them to try and get us some answers. Some useful information. I know you don't have much of a reason to trust me, but I'm asking you…as a friend, and as a friend of your mom's, to trust me. I've done nothing but help since I got here and that's all I want to continue doing."

In spite of how badly Tom wanted to punch the other man in the face, the same intuition that helped him ferret out liars urged him to accept Bishop's plea. He believed him, and although Tom knew there was still a side to him that was in the shadows, Bishop was the kind of man he needed by his side when they went up against the desperados. And if he was telling the truth about the radio, then he might also need his help as the mayor.

"Okay," Tom said with some reluctance. Handing the papers out to Bishop, he saw that there were several more like it scattered on the desk. "Have you managed to get any of those answers?"

"I'm afraid so," Bishop said with a sigh. "I was going to tell you about this tomorrow, anyway. I found out something you need to know. That everyone needs to know."

Tom braced himself for more bad news and wondered if there

would ever come a time again when things weren't so muddied. When right was right and wrong was wrong. When the sky was dark at night and the rain didn't kill anything.

"Jesper Duke's ranch is now a command center for the US military."

Tom closed his eyes and took a slow breath before opening them again. "Dillinger?"

Bishop shrugged. Tom had told him about the corporal, so he knew who he was referring to. "I didn't get many details, except it's clear they aren't stopping there. I'm afraid the fake quarantine isn't going to work for much longer, Tom. Sooner or later, there are going to be soldiers coming up the road."

Tom hoped that Bishop was telling him the truth about being on their side, because they were going to need all the help they could get. "Do we have any options?"

Bishop grinned, clearly relieved that Tom asked. "There are always options."

CHAPTER 22

G eneral Montgomery
Cheyenne Mountain Complex, Colorado

GENERAL MONTGOMERY STOOD FACING the giant map on his office wall, hands clasped behind his back. He'd spent so many hours staring at it that when the colors changed, lines shifted, and the landscape morphed into something altogether new, it was like watching an evolving season. It was changing again, and the red yarn strung along the West Coast was physically painful to look at.

"Hard to believe, isn't it?"

He twisted his shoulders a few inches so he could acknowledge Walsh, who was standing just inside the doorway to his office. "The continent is literally being molded into something new," Montgomery said with some reverence. "A third of the Oregon coast erased miles inland, the San Juan Islands in Washington submerged, and...tens of thousands dead in California.

We won't even know the extent of the latest damage there until we reestablish communication after the last storm."

"There's growing concern that the remaining tankers that were still in port have also been lost."

Montgomery winced. It was some of the largest stores of crude oil still accessible on the continent. It would be some time, of course, before anything could have been done with it, but at least they would have had the option. He hadn't even considered the impact of the hurricanes on the refineries. "Which ones?" he asked. "Washington or California?"

Walsh moved restlessly and cleared his throat. "All of them, sir."

General Montgomery turned back to his map. Although it was changing, it was still familiar enough to offer him a sense of control. If they could continue the information-gathering so he at least understood what was happening, he would be able to maintain order. Information was power and there was never a time when that was truer. "Why don't we have more updates?" he demanded, walking over to his desk where the latest reports were stacked. Picking up the top sheet, he waved it at Walsh like it was evidence of his inadequacies. "It's been nearly forty-eight hours since the last hurricane hit."

"Hurricane force winds receded only ten hours ago, sir, and the atmospheric interference increased to the point where communication was almost impossible all along the coast," Walsh explained. "We've been relaying messages successfully with eastern Washington, but they've only managed to get limited data themselves."

Montgomery slammed the paper back down on the desk. It was too early in the morning to argue and he hadn't even had his first cup of coffee. He knew he didn't need to lecture Walsh, but there was a long laundry list of bad news greeting him that morning and someone needed to answer for at least some of it.

"Tell me about 1st Recon," he demanded. Rubbing at his temple, the general picked up the mug of coffee that had already gone cold and sat down at his desk.

"We've had no further contact since they went dark last night," Walsh said, hesitating.

"Out with it, Colonel. I'm not in the mood to play twenty questions with you today."

"Alicia Jenson is a US governor. Why not simply set up a meeting with her?"

Montgomery stared at Walsh until the other man looked away. "I understand she now considers herself a senator. And are you going to make me explain the meaning of standing orders, Colonel? Is the continued destruction of our planet not enough evidence that we need to do whatever is necessary to ensure the survival of the people of the United States?"

Walsh cleared his throat again, and when he looked back up to meet Montgomery's eyes there was a hardness the general hadn't seen before. "I think, sir, that we are living in unusual times. It might be to everyone's benefit to try and work alongside the civilian government, rather than against them. Either that, or be bold enough to order her arrest instead of whatever game is being played."

Montgomery set his cup down and slowly pushed it off to the side before placing his hands on the desk. "You're sounding awfully mutinous this morning, Kelly."

Walsh swallowed hard at the use of his first name, though he didn't look away. "You've got it wrong, General. I'm doing my best to prevent insurrection, but you're making my job very hard lately. I just got word before coming here that one of the National Guardsmen at the gov—I mean, senator's estate was killed last night. There were eyewitness accounts of the recon unit and they're calling this a military operation. The state of Idaho is demanding answers immediately."

Montgomery's expression didn't change. He knew the mission could go one of several ways and was ready for them all. Ideally, it would have been a clean grab and the situation could have been more easily manipulated to their benefit. As it was, it would require more sacrifice, and that was still acceptable to him. "Issue a statement denouncing the 1st Force Reconnaissance team. Explain that they were ordered to disband after we investigated the botched mission in New Mexico. They've gone rogue and are now acting on their own accord."

Walsh's face reddened. "So, they're your scapegoat?"

"They are whatever we need them to be!" Montgomery barked as he jumped to his feet, causing Walsh to recoil. "It is imperative that we maintain authority or everything that we've managed to build will be lost. The rest of the people will be lost, Colonel, and that cannot...it *will* not happen. With Vice Admiral Baker and Senator Jenson out of the equation, their rebellion is effectively shut down and we can get back to rebuilding this country."

Walsh stood stiffly; his hands clamped into fists at his sides. Montgomery remained on his feet and watched his longtime friend carefully. He'd rather not detain him for treason, and the next minute would likely dictate whether the other man lived or died. It would be unfortunate, although better men had been sacrificed throughout history for the greater good.

A small sigh escaped the colonel's lips, and it reminded Montgomery of the last breath often heard before the soul left the body at the moment of death. "What's our next step then, sir?"

Relieved for the moment, but still wary of the colonel's loyalty, the general sat back down and resumed drinking his cold coffee as if the standoff hadn't happened. "Tell me about Dr. Watson's latest demands."

Walsh blinked once, and then twice, looking somewhat dazed. His brows furrowed and then relaxed as he realized they were moving on with business as usual. "Um, yes. She's still adamant that her granddaughter be allowed topside for more than an hour a day to get what she calls sunshine and fresh air."

"That's easy enough to make happen."

"Yes, General, I've already seen to it," Walsh replied, his voice still sounding weak as he continued to gather his wits. "The other request is a little harder to accommodate, though not without merit."

"Indoor farming." Montgomery lifted the report which listed the details. "She claims to have been part of a team that planned for potential events that limited the ability to grow food and raise cattle. Perhaps we've discovered why she was on the list."

"She's a geneticist," Walsh said, pointing out the obvious. "According to her, she was recently involved in a top-secret government program. Her role was to create genetically modi-fied seeds as part of a revolutionary seed vault here in the states."

"Comparable to Svalbard?" Montgomery asked. He didn't know much about the Svalbard global seed vault, except that it was called a doomsday vault and, much like Cheyenne, was located deep inside a mountain. Unfortunately, that mountain was on an arctic island in Norway. One of the reasons for its location was the cold. Even if the power in the vault failed, which it would have with the gamma ray, it would remain below freezing inside. Though there were some vaults in the US, with one of the largest being right there in Colorado, they were all susceptible to the repercussions of the flashpoint. The local one at the Colorado State University was housed in a regular build-ing. It was part of a massive fire and a total loss. Any others still accessible would be essentially useless, even if they had workable land to grow the seeds in.

"Better than Svalbard, and more than one."

The general paused with his cup halfway to his mouth. "More than one?"

Walsh's eyes narrowed. "You knew about this."

"What else did she say?" he demanded. Montgomery had allowed the colonel enough rope to hang himself with, but he wasn't about to start getting in the habit of explaining his motives to his assistant.

"She wants a team to help locate some appropriate caves and coordinate an indoor farming program." Walsh took a folded piece of paper from his back pocket. As he approached the desk and held it out to Montgomery, he could see that it was covered in a hand-written list. "Once we've met her requirements, she'll help us locate the vault."

"She doesn't know where it is?" Montgomery was alarmed.

"No, but she apparently knows someone who does," Walsh dropped the list and backed away like he was feeding a snake. "She said the different aspects of the project were kept separate in order to maintain a high level of secrecy, but she was friends with someone on the vault design team."

"Give her what she wants," Montgomery demanded, startling Walsh with the ease with which he gave the order. "I don't want anyone else talking to her, and isolate the team she puts together."

"Yes, sir."

"The communication that came in from Dillinger last night," General Montgomery said, moving on before Walsh tried to fish for more answers. "How was it sent?"

"Apparently there was a ham radio at the Pony Express station." Walsh scratched at his head, frowning. "Turns out they were even more organized than we thought."

"And this station is a farm on the outskirts of Helena, correct?"

The colonel nodded. "Yes, sir. The owner was killed in the raid, but as you can see by the report, Dillinger found evidence of several other similar stations, all connecting back to Mercy, Montana."

"This says he'll have a team in Mercy to confirm the quarantine is a hoax within a couple of days." Montgomery considered the importance of shutting down the supply line, the cattle, and strategic placement of another command outpost. Mercy might be just the kind of settlement they'd end up needing for the long-term. It was too bad they didn't have the 1st Force Reconnaissance at their disposal any longer. "Contact the colonel at Malmstrom. Have them ready a team to assist Dillinger." Malmstrom Air Force Base was about a hundred miles north of Helena, but could have troops in Mercy within a few days of receiving orders.

"Yes, sir. Anything else?"

Montgomery stared evenly at Colonel Walsh for several heartbeats. Some deadly things had been put on the table and they weren't easily swept aside. He knew his friend was looking for reassurance and he wasn't ready to give it to him. He pushed his mug to the edge of the desk. "Get me some fresh coffee."

Walsh struggled to keep a neutral expression as he took the cup and walked from the room without comment. When the door closed, the general rose and went back to his map. In spite of a bad start to the day, he was feeling much more optimistic.

Reaching out, Montgomery pulled the red stickpin that designated the town of Mercy. A smile that others might have mistaken for a sneer was his only outward expression as he replaced it with a green tack. "We'll find out soon enough what other secrets you're protecting," he whispered to the empty room.

CHAPTER 23

DANNY
Main Street, Mercy, Montana

THE SKY over Mercy was painted with a mosaic of intense colors as the sun rose slowly above the rooftops of Main Street. Danny rode right down the middle, staring up in awe as her horse tread lightly over the cracked blacktop that was already filling in with hardy weeds. A ragged, wispy line of auburn-colored clouds reached out from the east and ended like a bullseye at a building wall of clouds to the south. Twisting in her saddle to look behind her, Danny marveled at how the color seemed to flow from the sunrise to the storm and infuse it with some sort of supernatural energy.

Trying to shake off the sense of foreboding, she settled back in the saddle and called out to Grace to keep her close by, reassuring herself that everything would work out. Danny had just left her father back at the water station on the southern end of town. He'd continue to fulfill his role as water-hauler while she helped out at the ranch for the next few days. Glancing up at the sound of a neighing horse, she was relieved to see a large group of riders still gathered in front of city hall. Danny knew they would wait until after daybreak to leave, but she was still afraid of missing them. She wanted to make sure her father's medication was on the list of wanted items in the Pony Express riders' saddle bags. Her other reason was to say goodbye to Tom.

A rooster crowed from somewhere up the road, and she figured it must be one of the many inhabitants of the farmer's market. Danny had been through it once, briefly, and was amazed at how well organized it was. The bartering system was working well and she only heard one small disagreement that settled rather quickly. Her dad told her how it started with a few fruit stands and had rapidly grown to a large, covered area that spread from building to building across Main Street. It encompassed everything from small livestock, to all sorts of food items, and handmade goods like soap and toilet paper. Danny ended up trading a fish she'd caught for a couple of apples and a piece of pie. She already had plans for how she could contribute and gain from it.

Although it was early, a fair amount of people were already milling about. Danny was impressed with the tight-knit community and their willingness to work together. She had very limited knowledge of the town's politics, but even if Patty was right to step down as mayor when she did, there was no denying what she had helped to build. As Danny drew closer to the group, she wasn't surprised to see how many volunteers there were. Mercy was worth fighting for.

"Danny!" Tom called out when he spotted her, and she smiled at his enthusiasm. She wasn't sure when the shift occurred and she started to care so much about how he reacted to her, but it was an emotion she hadn't experienced in a very long time.

"I'm glad I didn't miss you," Danny said as he walked up. He reached out to stroke the horse's head in greeting and she saw how the mare immediately turned to him, wanting more attention. He definitely had a way with animals. Her dad said she was normally a skittish horse.

Danny was happy to see Chloe over talking with Bishop and Sheriff Waters. They could ride back to the ranch together. "Where's Ethan?" she asked when she didn't see the teen anywhere.

"He and Sam stayed back with my mom at the farm to get a jump on the hay," Tom explained. "It was so hot yesterday that I think they're looking forward to sweating a little less this morning."

Danny chuckled as Grace finished running around greeting everyone, and plopped herself down on Tom's feet. "She's going to miss you."

Tom knelt down and gave the retriever a hug, rubbing her head at the same time. "You take care of the farm, Grace." Grace barked once in response and then ran off again.

"I think that was a yes," Danny laughed. "We'll both watch over the farm, but only if you promise to come back soon."

Tom stood back up and looked as if he was going to say something, but Caleb intervened by slapping a large hand onto Tom's shoulder. Danny noticed he winced and wondered if the healing bullet wound was giving him any problems. "Just got a weird message from station one," Caleb said with some concern.

"Explain 'weird message'," Tom replied, rolling his shoulder slightly while he spoke.

"It's hard to explain," the older man said, frowning. "I sent my usual morning roll call and the response was basically the same as every other day, except that it wasn't."

Tom raised his eyebrows questioningly at Caleb, obviously wanting more of an explanation. Bishop and Sheriff Waters had just walked up in time to catch the gist of the conversation and the sheriff didn't look happy.

"Q-Code is essentially a type of Morse code shorthand for ham radio operators," Caleb said. "Just like with other forms of communication, each operator tends to develop their own recognizable tendencies and patterns. You know, shortening of words, dropping certain precursors and such." Caleb ran a hand over his head and huffed in frustration. "I can't exactly tell you how I know, but I don't think I'm talking to Henry anymore. I'd wager money someone else is on that radio, only they're trying to identify themselves as him."

Bishop looked first at the sheriff and then Tom. Danny immediately picked up on an added layer of tension as soon as Bishop joined them. She watched the silent exchange between him and Tom and knew it had to do with more than the news from Caleb. Tom's whole demeanor changed and the way he reacted to Bishop was like the old Tom, from when they were still out on the road. Actually, both men looked rather dangerous and Danny was suddenly more nervous about their planned attack.

"So, this special Morse code," Tom said, turning to Caleb. "What are the odds that someone randomly overrunning the station would know it?"

"That pretty much nails my main concern," Caleb said. "I've been an operator for a long time, but I started out in the Army. Whoever is using this Q-Code, chances are that they're military."

The comment drew another pointed look from Tom to Bishop and Sheriff Waters cleared his throat. "Mayor, how do you want to handle it?"

"Why don't you wait until Caleb can determine more?" Patty said, walking up to her husband. "I'm fully aware I'm not the mayor anymore, Tom, but I don't like this. You don't know what might be going on out there."

"No," Tom said adamantly. "We go now. We can't waste any

more time waiting for something that may or may not happen. If whoever is on the other end of the radio doesn't want us to know who they are, they certainly aren't going to tell us. The only way to be certain is to go there and check in on them."

"Isn't station one near Helena?" Danny asked, trying to remember what she'd heard about it over the past couple of days.

"Yes," Sheriff Waters confirmed. "A good two days' ride farther than where we're headed. I'll have some riders continue on with Jed to the station and cautiously scope it out."

"If the military is there, we'll bypass them for the next station," Tom said. "We can't let them destroy what you've worked so hard for. This supply line is working, and it's going to be critical to our chain of small communities in the coming months."

"Not you, Mayor," Sheriff Waters said gruffly. "You'll be needed here in Mercy. We have plenty of volunteers who can handle the task just as well."

Tom took his hat off and pursed his lips. It was obvious to Danny that he realized the sheriff was right and didn't want to admit it. "I knew there'd be reasons I'd regret accepting this role," he finally said, turning to Patty. "You sure you don't want the title back?"

Patty slipped an arm through Caleb's and grinned at Tom. "I'll be here to help you through the mounting paperwork when you get back, Mayor," she offered in reply.

"I'll keep trying to talk to him," Caleb said, turning away and taking Patty with him. "We'll be able to talk on the handhelds throughout the morning, until you're about ten miles south of town. I'll let you know if I learn anything."

"Come on," Sheriff Waters said to Bishop. "Let's go figure out who's going to ride on with Jed and make sure they have enough extra provisions for the trip."

"Can I take Grace inside with me?"

Danny turned to find Chloe standing behind her, holding on to Grace's collar. "Take her where?"

Chloe gestured to the city hall building. "In there. I need to talk to Caleb. Grace was way too interested in the chickens roaming around up the road."

"Sure," Danny said, amused. "Take your time. I was going to check out the market before we head to the ranch. We can meet there."

As Chloe ran up the steps with Grace, Danny was surprised when Tom took her arm and pulled her in the other direction. He didn't say anything until they were a couple of buildings away and he glanced back over his shoulder first. "I need to ask you a favor."

"Sure," Danny said without hesitation.

"There's a room in the loft of the barn." Putting an arm around her shoulders, Tom turned her so they had their backs to the group. "I can't explain why right now, but there's a ham radio up there. I need you to go through everything you can find. See if you can determine exactly what sort of information was being exchanged."

Danny's thoughts reeled. "What?"

"And then I need you to go through Bishop's things."

The connection was clear, and Danny thought she had an idea as to why there was a new tension between the two men. Turning slightly, she placed a hand on his shoulder and gave it a small squeeze. When he flinched, her eyes narrowed. "What happened, Tom?"

He turned so that they were facing each other, and he stared at her with an intensity that was both chilling and electrifying. "Do you trust me?"

"Of course," Danny answered without having to give it any thought. And she did, perhaps more than anyone aside from her own father. "I'd do anything for you, Tom."

There was no shy glance at her mouth or flustered, unsure gestures that time as Tom lowered his arm from her shoulders and wrapped it around her waist, pulling Danny against him. She felt his other hand at the back of her neck as he buried his fingers in her hair and drew her in for a long, passionate kiss.

Danny responded with a raw need that was only partially satisfied before his lips moved from her mouth and to where her jaw met the curve of her neck. "I promise to come back, Danny," he whispered before gently pushing away from her.

A strobe of lightning flickered in the distance as Tom took a step back, a physical ache replacing the heat of his touch. She fought her natural instinct to rebel against the intense emotions he was causing, refusing to allow herself to shut him—and the risk of being hurt—out. Perhaps, there in Mercy, Danny could do more than rediscover her passion for life. Maybe it was possible for her to find love.

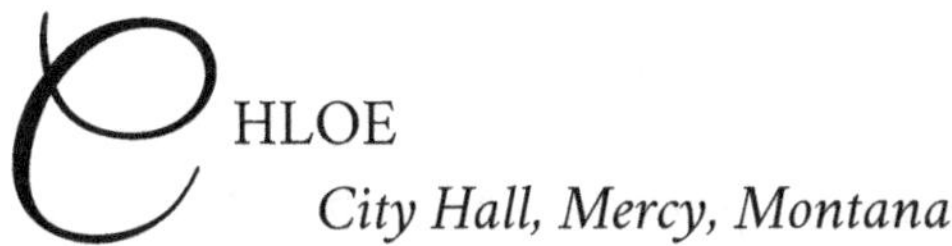

CHAPTER 24

CHLOE
City Hall, Mercy, Montana

CHLOE HAD BEEN in Mercy City Hall a few times, but never in the basement. After chasing Grace around a floor full of mostly empty offices, she found the basement access near the back of the building. As Chloe crept cautiously down the shadowy stairway, she admonished herself for every horror show she'd ever watched. Before the world went crazy, if anyone had suggested she'd be legitimately freaked out over a dark basement, Chloe would have laughed. Except, not much made sense anymore and she wasn't laughing.

At a turn in the second landing, the distant source of light became more apparent and Chloe sighed when she realized there were several solar lights set up. "Come on, Grace," she whispered to the dog, unsure why she was trying to be quiet. She had noticed that there was something about the lack of electricity in large buildings that compelled people to move carefully and speak quietly. It was an interesting phenomenon and she had some suspicions, but nothing solid. At the moment, it was purely fear.

"Hello?" Chloe called out when she reached the bottom and stepped out into a large, open room full of boxes and supplies. It was like the holy grail of the apocalypse and she was amazed the stuff wasn't under lock and key. Of course, there were probably only a few people who knew it was all kept there and most everyone was distracted at the moment with the posse out front.

Passing a stack of blankets and pillows, Chloe paused to look at a bag labeled "Toothbrushes". Since she hadn't had the nerve yet to tell Ethan his clothes weren't the only thing of his she'd been using, she bent over to see if there was one with a purple handle.

"Hello?"

Chloe jerked upright, a sparkly green toothbrush in her hand. "Oh!" She gasped in relief when she saw it was Patty. "Bishop told me Caleb still has his ham radio down here. I wanted to check in with him on the whole 'searching for parental survivors' quest."

Patty raised her eyebrows and looked at the implement in Chloe's hand, as Grace ran over to great her.

"Umm," Chloe blushed. "It might look like I was creeping around down here, trying to take things, but I honestly just happened to see this great big bag of toothbrushes and figured I could stop swapping spit unknowingly with Ethan."

Patty put a hand up to stop Chloe when she took a breath to continue. "It's fine, Chloe. You're welcome to it. And follow me. Caleb's radio room, as we've been calling it, is right over here."

Chloe shoved the toothbrush in her back pocket and eagerly followed the older woman. "Why is he down here?" she asked, trying to read the labels on the boxes they passed. She could really use some new underwear.

"Oh, he managed to rig up an antenna he's really happy with," Patty explained. She stepped aside as they approached the "room", where Caleb sat facing a desk, headset on and pencil in hand. He began tapping out some sort of message as they got close and the noise echoed through the cavernous space behind them. "That's the main reason he's chosen to stay down here," Patty continued, pulling a chair over for Chloe. "He claims he doesn't want to bother anyone, but I suspect it has more to do with not having anyone bother *him*. He'll spend hours scanning and listening, and he needs it to be quiet. Anything?" Patty asked when Caleb turned to acknowledge them, removing his headphones.

"Not from the station," he answered. "Caught a few more words from the weird one I was telling you about, though."

"Chloe was hoping for an update on the search for her parents," Patty said, gesturing to the teen.

Chloe took the offered seat and pulled her feet up under her. She'd been putting off asking any questions for days, because she was afraid of the answer. At first, she'd thought it would be better to simply not know. However, after spending some time with Ethan and seeing his reunion with his grandma, she'd been thinking more about her own parents.

"Any news?" Her voice sounded small and she cleared her throat. "I mean, I know you would have let me know if you heard something for sure…but, is there *anything*?"

Patty placed a hand on her shoulder and gave it a gentle, reassuring squeeze. "Tell her what you know, dear."

"I'm afraid it isn't much," Caleb said, pulling the headset the rest of the way down around his neck and giving Chloe his full attention. "My problem is that I don't know the proper channels the local government or military uses for Washington state. I put out a request locally with our military contact before we pretty much stopped talking to each other. I know they were going to be working on getting lists together, so I'm sure we'll hear from someone if there's a match."

Chloe tried to hide her disappointment by redirecting the conversation. "What's the weird one?"

"Huh?" Caleb asked, thrown off by the change in subject.

"You mentioned a weird message to Patty. What's that about?"

Caleb shrugged and picked up a piece of paper that was sitting in front of him. "I spend a lot of time scanning, but with all the atmospheric interference, I don't get much. It limits the range, which means it's even more important to be on the right channel to hear anything."

"It's not talking, though, right?" Chloe asked, genuinely interested. "It's, like, just a tapping sound?"

Caleb smiled, and nodded. Grace approached him then and set her head in his lap, provoking a deep, rumbling chuckle from the man. As he rubbed at her ears, he surprised Chloe by handing the sheet of paper to her. "That's correct. With the damage to the atmosphere it's impossible to get a voice transmission out. I don't know if we'll ever be able to establish that type of communication, other than by setting up a crapload of repeaters, which is what we've been planning to do."

Chloe took the paper and looked at him questioningly before reading it. "What do you mean?"

"We've got several other smaller communities we've managed to unite, in a way, through our Pony Express. Eventually, we'll need to increase our trading and exchange of goods and information and when the quickest way to say hello is by horse, things take way too long. We got our main station out by Helena set up with a radio a local there had, but that's it. Once Tane managed to successfully get a repeater working here above Mercy, we began planning how to place a string of them between our valleys."

"Seems like a good plan," Chloe said, impressed.

"To talk about it, you'd think it's a marvelous idea," Caleb agreed. "But when it comes down to the logistics of first building these repeaters, and then figuring out where and how to place them to make them work, it turns into something nearly impossible."

"Thankfully, Bishop's been helping," Patty added. "He's been such a blessing. He's incredibly knowledgeable in so many areas."

"Huh," Chloe grunted as she glanced down at the paper in her hand. It was a jumble of words that didn't really seem to make any sense. "What is this, and what makes it weird?" she asked, giving it a shake.

"It was strong," Caleb said simply.

"What do you mean?" Chloe still didn't get why that made it interesting.

"One of those signals, the one who signs off with 'B', is close enough for me to easily pick it up when scanning, although I've only heard parts of two transmissions now."

"How close?" Chloe asked, her interest piqued.

"Closer than the Pony Express station, but it's impossible really to say where. I figure it's coming from a private radio operator somewhere within a hundred-mile radius of here."

"This doesn't seem to really say anything," Chloe said, frowning at the seemingly random words.

"Yeah," Caleb agreed. "I think that was the end of a one-sided transmission. Whoever they were talking to didn't answer. The other one was slightly more fascinating."

"Can I see it?" Chloe asked. She wasn't sure why, but she felt compelled to see more.

Caleb smiled good-naturedly and began flipping through a notebook. "I keep everything filed by date," he explained. "It was about a week ago. Ah! Here it is."

Chloe accepted the document and then leaned back in the chair. As she read through it, the sense of unease she'd begun to experience intensified. Sitting up straighter, she read it a second time:

ALL SAFE. ARRIVED AT OFFICE. – H
CURRENT STATUS OF FARM? WILL RENDEZVOUS WHEN ABLE. – B
FARM AT TTT SECURE. WILL STAND BY. – H
HARD COPY. – B

HER STOMACH SUDDENLY SOUR, Chloe fought against placing all of the various pieces of the puzzle into place. She didn't want to see the completed image. Except her brain didn't work that way. She was gifted, as her teachers called it. Only Chloe wasn't feeling especially gifted at that moment, sitting there in the shadowy basement under Mercy, holding what was likely something only she and a couple of other people would understand. Because she knew Hicks, and she knew he'd been going to the Trek Thru Trouble office. And she knew Bishop.

Or did she?

CHAPTER 25

RUSSELL

Henry's Hollow, Near Mercy, Montana

THE OPENING to the mine in the side of the hill was unimpressive and Russell paused at the threshold, wondering if the exertion would be worth it. Glancing back over his shoulder, he took in the dreary scene behind him. The field housing the natural spring had been transformed from a picturesque landscape to a muddy pit with a rough-looking shack in the middle of it.

The builders were calling it a water shed, and were quite pleased with it. They'd even made a sign to hang over the door. The sloping road and area in front of the shed had been turned into a quagmire by the wagons coming and going during and after the storms moving through. They'd begun to use pavers someone found in an attempt to build a road, but Russell wasn't impressed with their progress so far.

Where others saw an accomplishment of great proportions, Russell saw yet another vain attempt to control something not meant to be controlled. The thought buoyed his resolve and he turned back to the tunnel with more vigor. If what they'd said about Henry's Hollow in the meeting was true, he might have found his exodus strategy.

It was getting late in the afternoon and the last water run of the day had just left. They were shorthanded at the spring for several reasons, so Russell had volunteered to help out. The other woman overseeing the loading process rode out with the last wagon, and when Russell found himself alone at the spring, it was the perfect opportunity to explore.

Twenty feet in, the slant downward was enough to cut off most of the light offered by the opening and so Russell took a solar lamp from his pocket. The solar panels were an interesting phenomenon. So long as the devices weren't hooked up to a battery when the gamma ray tore through the planet, they were unharmed. Ironic, really.

Holding the rather weak light out in front of him, Russell studied the rotting wooden support beams with a critical eye. Lode mining was a dangerous occupation that took off in Montana around the turn of the century, and there weren't many that operated in the area beyond the 1950s. At least, that was what Dr. Olsen told him when he'd inquired about the local history that morning.

True to how it was depicted, the tunnel branched off a hundred feet in and Russell followed the smaller passageway to the left. He could immediately see a haze of faint daylight a short distance ahead. Encouraged, he continued toward it and in less than five minutes found himself standing at the opening to what could only be described as a grand cavern.

Russell estimated it to be the size of two football fields and at the apex was seventy-five feet tall. There were two openings in the roof of the structure that the fire chief had called chimneys. They allowed in enough light that Russell could see a fair amount of the chamber. Stalactites hung down in the farthest reaches, where water slowly worked its way down from the chimneys and dripped into small pools on the far side of the cave.

Turning in a half-circle, he envisioned it as the industrious townspeople did: covered in rich soil and eventually turning into a sea of wheat or hay. Russell tsked as the image faded and was replaced instead with the hollow as it was meant to be, free of mankind's influence and interference. Only, it was already marred by the remnants of Mercy's original settlers.

Stepping carefully down on to the floor of the cave, Russell studied the rusting tools scattered near his feet. A broken wooden cart lay on its side amongst them, its usefulness long faded. A large boulder close to the artifacts was partially defaced by the graffiti of the modern-day Mercy teens who were proud to leave their mark.

Disgusted by the blatant disrespect, Russell turned from the rock and ignored the relics, heading for a stack of crates farther back in the shadows. His pulse quickened as he saw the faded markings on the sides of the wooden boxes. The fire chief and Sheriff Waters had been right, there was an alarming amount of old dynamite.

Counting the crates, Russell discovered there was a total of ten that supposedly weighed fifty pounds each. Not all of them were obviously sweating, but enough were to make it impressive that none of the obnoxious kids entering the cave over the years had blown themselves up.

Some of the crates were open and a few sticks were displaced, so Russell imagined an extra element of danger to entering the cave was the dare to touch the dynamite. Fortunately for the kids, the nearest ones hadn't degraded to the point that any chemicals had sweated out of it to then crystalize into a highly volatile substance.

Cautiously, Russell walked around the boxes and spotted one

at the bottom near the back that was covered in the telltale clumps of whitish material. He took a measured step back and then went over to some of the other discarded materials. After only a few minutes of searching, he found what he was after; a large roll of detonating cord. It was pretty typical to store both the explosives and cord together, so he wasn't surprised, although it was a relief. He would have been able to rig something else, but having the cord made everything so much easier.

The nice thing about dynamite was that it really hadn't changed much in over a hundred years of use. It was essentially an absorbent material soaked in nitroglycerin. As an explosive, the older it was, the less stable it became and was easier to detonate. It had been over twenty years since Russell first learned about dynamite, though it wasn't something you easily forgot.

After running away from home as a teen, he had experienced several different jobs. The one he'd stayed with the longest was a large and prosperous logging company. He didn't have his CDL and couldn't drive a truck, but he eventually worked his way up to a hooktender and it paid good money. Enough to get him started in college after a few years. In those early months on the job, he was basically a mule for whatever needed to be done. The initial phase of a clear-cut was to make a road, and in order to carve a road into the side of a mountain, you needed dynamite. A lot of dynamite. Russell may not have been certified to handle it, but he did everything else, and he learned. He always learned.

While he didn't have the knowledge to determine the yield of the explosion that would be caused by five hundred pounds of dynamite, any idiot could figure out it would be big. More than big. It would be *massive*.

An added benefit of the old dynamite was that he wouldn't have to rig the detonator cord directly to the blasting caps. There was enough unstable material there that all it needed was one trigger. The cord was a high-speed fuse, but it would still take long enough to burn through the whole line so that he'd have time to get to a safe enough distance.

"How far away is safe?" Russell asked the empty cavern. Rubbing at his chin, he tilted his head and looked up at the chimneys, considering the depth of the chamber. The mountain was already riddled with tunnels, weakening it. At the least, he figured the spring would easily be destroyed and anyone near it, killed. At best, the blast could bring the whole mountainside down, the resulting landslide burying up to half the town.

The new mayor's vigilante brigade wouldn't be back for at least two days and then everyone would be busy getting ready for the town barbeque on the Fourth of July. Russell grinned and started whistling the national anthem. While there wouldn't be any bombs bursting in the air, he could certainly give them a memorable show.

Taking the detonator cord, he hid it under the remains of the old cart. It wasn't likely that anyone else would be in the cave in the next couple of days but there was no need to be careless. He'd hate to lose the useful material.

Wiping his hands off on his jeans, Russell took one last fleeting look at Henry's Hollow and felt a strong sense of synchronicity. It was something he'd experienced occasionally throughout his life, typically when he first met one of his victims. Lately, it was on a grander scale.

His eyes bright with excitement, Russell reluctantly backed out of the cavern. He had a funeral to officiate.

CHAPTER 26

*J*AMES
> Master Sergeant, US Marines, 1*st* Force Reconnaissance
>
> *Somewhere in Central Montana*

THE BLADES of the helo slowly rotated behind them as the motor whined down, kicking up dirt and debris from the abandoned highway. After a long night of waiting for the sun to rise so they could get over the mountains, the rugged group of soldiers and lone diplomat made it to their destination on barely more than fumes.

James squinted up at the tree-covered mountains of the Lewis and Clark National Forest. Although he'd hiked and camped in them for most of his life, it was always awe-inspiring. Even more so when you were dropped into the middle of them in a sputtering helicopter.

"Moving him has opened the wound back up," Flores directed to James. He was helping Hawk limp down the road and a fresh trickle of blood was oozing through the gauze wrapped around his calf. The corporal looked around at the uninhabited land-scape. "I'd really like to get a few stitches in this, sooner than later."

Senator Jenson glanced at her head of security and put a hand out in front of James. When he only slowed but didn't stop, her face clouded with anger. "Stop!" she shouted, while planting her feet and stubbornly blocking his way. "You need to start giving me some answers, Sergeant. I don't even know where we are and I've left behind all—" Her voice caught and she looked away from James, clenching her jaw and staring at the large pine trees hugging the road.

James exchanged a look with Jay and then Lucas. Corporal Lance and Sergeant Lee had stayed back with the pilot to guard the helicopter on the off chance anyone armed tried to approach it. He'd intentionally landed a few miles away from his target for that reason, although so far, even with the loud arrival there wasn't another soul to be seen.

Emotional conversations weren't his forte and James had avoided speaking with the woman as much as possible. But she had a point and he knew the senator deserved some sort of explanation. "For now, our mission is to locate my father and then get you both to a safe place. From there, we'll work on getting your family."

"And we're accomplishing that by flying around the skies of Montana until we run out of gas?" the senator retorted, clearly unimpressed with the plan.

James had refused to tell her or Hawk where they were headed. The ex-soldier understood why, but the senator was a harder sell. It was for the same reason his own men were often left out of the details of an assignment. If something went sideways, there was less chance of any sensitive information getting out. In this case, James was trying to protect the suspected location of his dad. It was something General Montgomery sought, and he would do anything necessary to prevent the general from getting it. If that meant having to babysit an irate senator, James could live with that.

"That building we saw from the air is a couple more miles up ahead," James explained, moving around Senator Jenson and motioning for his men to follow. "It belongs to an organization my father volunteered for and there's a good chance that's where he was when the gamma ray hit. I found information that indicated he was on vacation during the event and I know he had plans to come here sometime this summer."

"What makes you think he'd still be there?" Hawk asked. Though he was pale and clearly in pain, he was still moving and James was impressed with his resilience.

"Because it's what I would have done," he said simply. "For whatever reason, he doesn't want to be found. I know my dad. For him to still be dark, it either means he's dead or else it's intentional. If it's the latter, I think we'll find him here. The office is isolated, remote, and likely well-stocked with survival gear. It's a good place for someone who doesn't want to be found."

"Except by someone who would know he's there," Senator Jenson said thoughtfully. "And if he was on that list and already on General Montgomery's radar, then I'm guessing he was already under some intense scrutiny prior to the flashpoint. What makes you think you're the only one who knows about this place?"

James glanced over at the senator and raised his eyebrows in silent approval. "I knew better than to ask why, but the time my dad spent here was off the grid. He worked under an alias and I'm pretty sure he covered any trace of his involvement."

"And this was normal to you?" the senator asked, rolling her shoulders.

James chuckled. "I didn't know what normal was until I was

old enough to understand that my friend's families were different. My dad's been in the military my whole life and worked special ops, including black, since I was a kid. I learned early on not to ask questions, because they wouldn't be answered."

"And if he isn't here?" Hawk asked. "What then? Because that bird isn't going to take us much farther unless you happen to have some jet fuel lying around out here somewhere."

"It might be a good place to lie low for a few days," James said. "I know the area, and we aren't far from Malmstrom Air Force base. I've got some potential contacts there."

Senator Jenson nodded and looked somewhat relieved. "Okay. That's a beginning, at least."

"You think they got a decent field kit at this place?" Flores asked, handing Hawk off to Lucas to get a break.

"It's a survivalist outfit that takes people on long treks," James explained. "I'm pretty sure they've got some advanced first aid gear."

James caught a flicker of movement off to his left, a shadow moving in between a stand of ponderosa pines. Without reacting, he casually moved his right hand out away from his body and made a slight motion to Jay. His friend responded with a mere nod of his head and then slowed his step until he was several paces behind James.

When the movement came again, the two men reacted as one, swinging their rifles around simultaneously toward the potential threat. "Show yourself!" James bellowed, his deep voice echoing through the valley.

"James?"

James pivoted around to face the opposite side of the road, where the new voice had originated. Moving agilely from the woods was a man he recognized, and a brief flash of anticipation blossomed in his chest until he forced the emotional reaction down. He knew the soldier, but his being there didn't make any sense.

"You can stand down, Sergeant," the man said with authority, his hands weaponless and out to his side. "It's okay, Adam!" he shouted. "Ben! You guys can come out." James shifted slightly to observe two teen boys emerge from the trees. "We're cool here. Right, James?"

James studied the rugged appearance of the man. He was wearing hiking clothes that were torn and dirty, but his face and hair looked recently washed. Though he'd clearly been roughing it, his face wasn't sallow or haggard like so many other survivors they'd seen over the past few weeks.

His name was Captain Brandon Hampton. He was an intelligence officer who had worked for his father for the past four years. James had only met him a few times as he and his father had become more distant, but the fact that the captain was there was both encouraging and confusing.

James lowered his M4 the rest of the way and motioned for his men to do the same. The teens appeared to be unarmed and had come to stand behind Hampton, glancing nervously at the soldiers. "What are you doing here, Ha—"

"Hicks," the captain interrupted, his eyes narrowing as he stared steadily at James. "I'm just called Hicks when I'm volunteering out here with the kids."

Some more of the pieces fell into place for James then, but the only outward sign of his revelation was that he stood a little straighter and his eyes widened for a fleeting moment. Though he had always suspected the Trek Thru Trouble was a front for something, he couldn't imagine what it was. That it was somehow connected to his dad being on the list hadn't been a consideration until then, and James silently chastised himself for not being more perceptive. However, they had all still somehow managed to be there at that moment, and he knew it was more than just a coincidence.

"You know why I'm here," James said simply, and waited for the rest of their quest to be fulfilled.

Hicks smiled then and ran a hand over his head, clearly relieved. "You can't possibly know how happy I am to see you guys," he offered before taking several steps closer to James. Once in front of him, he crossed his arms over his chest and looked up with an expression of determination. "I know where your father is, James. If you'd like, I can take you there. It's a place called Mercy."

CHAPTER 27

TOM

South of Mercy, Montana

THE PERSISTENT FEELING that he was missing something wouldn't allow Tom to relax. Even though it was past dusk and the shadows were moving in, he continued to pace along the edge of the road with a nervous energy he wasn't accustomed to.

"Here."

Tom turned to find Bishop holding out a steaming cup of coffee, his expression hard to read. The two of them hadn't spoken much since the night before, leaving things at a sort of uneasy truce until they could get beyond the current situation. Tom didn't regret asking Danny to look through his things, but he hoped he was wrong. If for no other reason than his mother's sake, although the man was undeniably beneficial to have around.

He accepted the drink and then scrutinized the fire burning in their camp. "It could be bigger," he commented. Walking past

Bishop, he bent to pick up a couple of sticks and then tossed them on the fire.

They'd arrived that afternoon to where the trail they suspected the desperados used intersected with the freeway. The real Pony Express riders, Barry and Jed, broke off from the group a mile in advance, while the rest of them hung back and dispersed evenly into the woods. There were eleven of them total, including two of the sheriff's deputies, and three men and one woman volunteer. They were all well-armed, and with the element of surprise, shouldn't have an issue overpowering the other, more ragged gang.

When they failed to encounter anyone on the road, Tom sent one of the deputies ahead to scout for several miles. He returned an hour later without coming across any signs of their assailants lying in wait.

Since it was obvious there wasn't an ambush already set up for them, they moved on to plan B. Bishop and Tom made an obvious camp a short distance past the trail with a large fire to advertise their location. If no one took the bait by late morning, they'd go ahead and make a direct assault on the outlaws' camp. While he'd rather draw them out, Tom had no problem taking the fight to them. Except...his intuition was causing him to replay the various scenarios in his head, looking for the factor that his subconscious was screaming at him to notice.

"We're supposed to look like unsuspecting Pony Express riders, not idiots dancing around a bonfire," Bishop muttered. He stomped past Tom and sat down on a rotting log. "What's the matter with you? Sit down."

Tom clenched his jaw and forced himself to stop moving. He was well aware the rest of their men were listening, concealed nearby in the woods. Squatting a couple of feet away from Bishop, he took a long gulp of coffee before finally looking at him, and spoke in a low voice. "Something doesn't feel right."

Tom expected the older man to laugh or ridicule him in some way. Instead, Bishop stood slowly and took a long look around. Without commenting, he unclipped the radio from his belt. "Waters, this is Bishop. Status?"

It was the sheriff's idea to bring two radios so they could communicate with each other over short distances. So far, it was working well. He was staked out with one of his deputies just north of the trail.

"We're status—stand by."

Tom and Bishop looked at each other, the tension building.

"We've got a rider!" Sheriff Waters whispered. *"One rider approaching the road from the trail."*

"Let him go," Bishop barked into the radio as he moved toward the fire. He waved his other arm at the nearby trees to signal the men to start moving. "Help me put this out," he said calmly to Tom.

Tom was again left with an impression of a man who had done more than served briefly in the military, but he didn't have time to mull over those implications. Instead, he joined Bishop in kicking the dirt they'd stockpiled on the fire, successfully smothering it.

Jed and Barry ran across the highway with Deputy Moore, so that both sides of the road would be covered. Tom and Bishop stood in the middle, rifles in hand, and Tom could already hear the horse approaching at a decent pace.

"Just the one," Sheriff Waters' voice squawked from the radio at Bishop's waist.

Tom frowned. Only one rider? Odds were that he was one of the desperados, since he came from the trail, but it was entirely possible it was someone else.

As horse and rider became visible in the gathering darkness, Tom raised his rifle. "Law enforcement! Stop and identify yourself!"

The clopping of the horse's hooves stuttered and then stopped as the rider pulled up hard, nearly unseating himself. Tom could tell right away that he was a young and inexperienced rider.

"Get off the horse," Bishop ordered, not allowing any room for introductions or pleasantries.

The man shifted in his saddle and his horse took a few voluntary steps forward, making his face more visible. Tom was surprised to discover he wasn't much older than Ethan, though his hardened expression was full of hate and loathing. "Why in the hell would you think I'm going to listen to you?" He held both of his hands low at his sides, so that they weren't visible.

"Jason?"

Tom glanced sideways at Bishop, surprised by the tone of his voice and the fact that he seemed to know the kid's name. Confused, he wavered slightly in his concentration and it was the opening Jason was looking for.

Kicking his horse, the teen leaned forward at the same time and raised his right hand up to level a gun in their direction. The mare charged, her eyes wild, as Jason shot randomly at them.

Tom leaped out of the way, unable to clearly aim past the horse. Rolling once as two more rounds exploded nearby, he came up on a knee and brought the rifle around. With the boy in his sights, Tom hesitated. Taking revenge by shooting a teenager in the back while he fled wasn't something he could ever resort to. Lowering the weapon, he looked over to confirm Bishop was okay and was surprised to see him take off running down the road.

"Jason!" Bishop yelled, sprinting faster.

Tom quickly followed and noticed how the boy was leaning sideways in the saddle. Jason only made it twenty more feet before falling to the ground, where he lay unmoving. The horse continued to trot away but eventually stopped, her sides heaving as she stomped at the blacktop.

Sheriff Waters and his deputy came galloping down the road, and he took the scene in before reholstering his pistol. "No other riders so far!" Waters called out.

Bishop had already rolled the boy over by the time Tom caught up and it was obvious he had suffered a fatal wound. A section of his neck was torn open, and blood pooled rapidly under him as he bled out.

"You know him?" Tom asked, trying to piece it all together.

Bishop nodded, his face stoic. "Yes. He was one of the boys from my original hiking group. His name is Jason."

Tom couldn't fathom how a teenager who had started out on a week-long survival excursion could have ended up with a group of killers targeting Mercy. "Wait," Tom said, remembering one of his mom's stories. "Is this the same guy you caught up at the lake? The one who tried to steal the horses?"

"He's also the one who attempted to rob me," Jed confirmed as he joined them. "I'm sorry if I killed him, Bishop. He was shooting at you. I didn't think I had much choice."

Bishop held a bloody hand up to stop Jed from saying anything else. "Yeah, Tom. It's him." Staring intently at Jason for a moment, Bishop let go of his shoulders and then stood. "He's gone." He looked back to where the sheriff sat on his horse. "He's obviously not a one-man posse. He's doing something else out here."

"Bishop, I—"

"You have nothing to apologize for," Bishop said, interrupting Jed. "He chose this." He pointed at the dead teen and the horse that was slowly walking back to them. "Life is all about the choices we make. I tried to get that simple message through to him in the few days we were together, but he wasn't willing to listen."

Tom was trying not to compare Jason to his own son, and some of the choices they'd all been faced with since the world fell apart. He was struck by the feeling that this connection with the boy and Bishop and the ranch all led to something more.

The mare approached him, and Tom wondered if it had been stolen from their other riders. Taking a rein, he gave her a cursory glance to make sure she wasn't shot, before noticing the saddle bags. The markings on the bag confirmed it belonged to their Pony Express, but Tom was more concerned with what might be inside them. Bishop was right; the kid was out there for a reason. Pulling the leather satchel off the horse, he dumped its contents on the ground.

Aside from a knife, water, and some food, the only other item of interest was a curious-looking envelope. It was a large, manila envelope with block writing in the top left corner:

COMMAND CENTER TWO

DUKE RANCH

Tom's breath quickened as he opened it and pulled out a torn, half-sheet of paper. The lettering on it was much rougher than that on the envelope. He struggled to see it in the fading light, but the simple correspondence was painfully clear as he read it out loud for everyone to hear.

"Orders received. We accept the terms. Cattle will be delivered as instructed on Miner's Trail. Leaving now." Tom's voice cracked as the meaning of the letter sank in.

"There's something on the other side," Bishop pointed out.

Turning the sheet over, Tom realized that the outlaws must have simply torn off the lower half of the original correspondence to answer it. The name neatly printed just below the crease shouldn't have been a surprise. "Dillinger," he growled, crumpling the paper up in his hand.

Of course. That was the connection he'd missed and should have realized the night before when Bishop told him about the

Duke Ranch. They'd found the maps he and Jesper Duke had spent an evening poring over and marking routes on. Dillinger had already known about Mercy and Jason knew exactly where the farm and cattle were.

"He was just a messenger," Bishop said, mirroring Tom's thoughts.

What had he done?

Tom reeled away from the other men and began to run for Lilly.

Life was all about choices.

Tom leapt onto Lilly's back and they set off up the darkening road at a gallop. Even if she ran all night, they might not get there in time.

Bishop was right. Tom had made the choice to seek revenge under the guise of protecting the town, and in doing so had left them vulnerable. While they'd been riding away from the people they loved, the desperados were already heading toward them.

The fight for Mercy was about to begin, and it would start with an attack on Miller Ranch.